DETERMINE YOUR ⌐

THE YOUNG MASTERS OF TIME

YOU ARE THE HERO OF THIS BOOK!

WRITTEN BY
JEFF STORM

ILLUSTRATED BY
HARVEY CHAN

EDITED BY
KAROLINA BRYNCZKA

CCB Publishing
British Columbia, Canada

The Young Masters of Time, Determine Your Destiny No. 3:
You Are the Hero of This Book!

Copyright ©2016 by Jeff Storm
ISBN-13 978-1-77143-287-0
First Edition

Library and Archives Canada Cataloguing in Publication
Storm, Jeff, 1972-, author
The young masters of time, determine your destiny no. 3 : you are the hero
of this book! / written by Jeff Storm ; illustrated by Harvey Chan. -- First edition.
ISBN 978-1-77143-287-0 (pbk.).--ISBN 978-1-77143-288-7 (pdf)
Additional cataloguing data available from Library and Archives Canada

Illustrations and cover artwork by: Harvey Chan

Publisher: CCB Publishing
British Columbia, Canada
www.ccbpublishing.com

YOUNG READERS' REVIEWS
of *Petrified World*, the 1st book in the
DETERMINE YOUR DESTINY series

"I read *Petrified World*. What I loved about it is that the book was so much fun for kids and exciting in every way! I want to read *No Return Land*. It is so fascinating how you can flip through the sections again and again. I love that I could restart the story." - *Alicia, 9 years old*

"*Petrified World* is my favourite thing to read! You get to choose cool powers, what to do and where to go. I'm sure the next books will also be so awesome!" - *Korina, 11 years old*

"I read *No Return Land* and loved it! It is full of adventure, has super cool pictures, and it's hard to win! It's super cool how you can pick different sections to read, and different skills to win! So are you ready for a super cool adventure...and will you survive?"
- *Talissa, 10 years old*

"*Petrified World* is a powerful book that is packed with action and suspense! This amazing book makes me wonder what will happen to me in the adventures ahead." - *Maja, 12 years old*

"I enjoyed reading *Petrified World*, very clever concept. Great introduction, entire story was well thought out. After each decision the story became even more exciting!" - *Mack, 14 years old*

"These books are really action-packed! They are very exciting and require a lot of hard decisions. There is an amazing introduction that explains very well who you are, and what your mission is. The outcome of what happens is completely in your hands. I highly recommend these books to everyone!" - *Samuel, 11 years old*

"*Petrified World* and *No Return Land* are exploding with excitement and action! YOU choose your path and YOU are the hero! I immediately found myself in another world. Loved it!"
- *Eddie, 10 years old*

"Simply amazing! I am so impressed with Jeff Storm's books. A real delight!" - *Julia, 15 years old*

"I feel that Jeff Storm's books are the best for kids because they inspire us to be heroes." - *Megan, 11 years old*

"*Petrified World* and *No Return Land* are the best! You are the hero and there are also different cool magical worlds in which you get to defeat wacky villains! Jeff Storm is amazing! I really loved leaping into fantasy worlds with fun characters!" - *Jack, 10 years old*

"I think Jeff's books are amazing! They are not like ordinary adventure books! I hated reading but now, I love it...and I am the hero every time!" - *Mike, 13 years old*

"Both books are great! I love the amazing illustrations and how well the books are crafted! The character's descriptions are unique and make the stories so alive!" - *Omar, 11 years old*

"Jeff Storm puts so much effort into his books by making everything so detailed, which is exactly why I love his books! Every word in each book is so precise and well chosen. I can't wait to read the next one!"
- *Pia, 10 years old*

"I really like the *Determine Your Destiny* books! I think that so many characters like Zenkay and Darkblade are so cool! I am so glad that I could read books that are just like a video game. These books are very detailed and have many great choices to choose from. I am looking forward to reading all of Jeff Storm's books!" - *Carissa, 10 years old*

This book is dedicated to all the brave warrior readers
daring to jump into this great adventure,
especially my children Johan and Paulina.

As well, to my wonderful wife Karolina:
thank you for your initial and ongoing support,
for believing in me and for your marketing savviness.

Good luck to all!

Your mission is no easy task but
challenge your imagination
in order to complete this magical journey!

HOW TO READ THIS BOOK

This is no ordinary book, which you simply read by flipping the pages one after the other. You will travel throughout this book, going back and forth to complete your mission. At the end of almost every section, you will have to make a choice regarding what you want to do or where you want to go next. Only YOU can make such decisions, but you must know that every one of your choices can be either excellent or fatal for you. If you die, your mission officially ends. At that point, in order to continue your mission, you can either start reading the book from the beginning again, or simply go back to the section before you died, and make a better choice this time.

Your mission is no easy task, so get ready to rumble and fight for those who need your help…and…at the same time…try to stay alive!

YOUR STORY

Everybody has a story to tell. But your story is like no other. It is almost from another world. This story is in every molecule of your body and has changed your life forever. It will stay in your soul for eternity…It is who you were destined to become and who you will always be.

It started years ago. You were on your way home, coming back from a trip to China, on board flight 779. Abruptly, your plane tipped forward and started to free-fall above Tibet. You were sitting right by the window, next to the wing, and with horror, you noticed the burning engines. But it was too late to panic. Within seconds, a terrible shock split the plane right open, crushing it, pulverizing almost everything inside, killing the crew members and the passengers, and ejecting you out of the aircraft into the freezing night. Before you could realize what was happening, you were thrown down the side of an icy mountain, and sliding down the steep peak at tremendous speed. Blinded by the blowing snow hurting your eyes, you suddenly crashed against an enormous rock, fracturing the back of your skull. Then nothing. Only darkness.

The next morning, by means of incredible luck, you were found almost dead by a group of Tibetan monks. On an improvised stretcher, they rushed you inside their lamasery to try to save you…and they did. You were in a coma for a month, but when you finally woke up, you had no memory! Your name, where you came from, everything about you was a deep mystery. The lamasery's High Priest said you could stay until you regained your memory. So you stayed…nine long years!

During those years, you slowly regained your memory, learned to speak Tibetan, and became one of the few privileged people to earn the right to learn various mystical Tibetan arts. You mastered many healing arts, martial arts, and magical arts. Having learned the basics of all magical arts, the High Priest asked you to specialize in five of those arts, telling you that you would master all the other magical arts with time and experience. He also told you to use what you have learned for good purposes only.

You will always clearly remember the last words the High Priest said to you:

"You have acquired extremely rare and amazing skills. It has now become your destiny to preserve all real life forms, and to help those in need. You must know that if an object is given life through a magic spell, it is not a real life form; therefore if it attacks you, you can destroy it."

He also told you:

"You must defend your own life or someone else's if it is threatened. With the powers and skills you possess, you can neutralize your opponents using the least amount of force required in order to preserve their life. If your opponent is not a real life form, do what you have to stay alive and protect others. Now go in peace."

After receiving his blessing and thanking him and all the monks for what they had done for you, it was time for you to go back home. You embraced everyone and promised you would be back some day to visit them. Then, trying to hide your extreme feelings of sadness while holding back a tear, you left to your former life…but you would never forget your Tibetan family.

You knocked on your parents' door. It was New Year's Day. You will always remember the look on your mother's face when she saw you standing in the doorway. The house, full of family and friends, went dead silent when they heard your mother's reaction. Then, they all rushed to the main door...and saw you! Suddenly, nothing but screams, tears of joy, shouts, frenetic hugs, and kisses. Emotions ripped through the air while you were hugged by everyone. That New Year's Day was the best one for your family, and your mother said she would have never expected, in a million years, to receive such a wonderful gift from the universe.

After entering the house and being bombarded with questions, you told your family and friends what had happened to you during the past nine years. However, you chose not to say anything about your special training, skills, and powers. You felt they would not understand. Maybe you will tell them some day.

So this is your story. But it is only the beginning…

YOUR MISSION

In the smallness of our world, the curious human being has always wondered: "What if it was possible to travel back in time?" So far, Science has demonstrated that time travel is not possible, that such a concept is pure science fiction.

Everybody knows that the present is now and that the past was before, leaving only a trail of memories and experiences behind it. Our past actions and decisions always affect the present in good or bad ways. This is why sometimes we wish we could go back in time to do some things differently, to fix a bad choice we have made or simply to relive a beautiful moment. Nevertheless, the past only exists in our mind, on pictures, in history books...

...or does it?

In our world, very few people have heard of the akashic records...but these records do exist! They represent a virtual video library of everything that has ever happened in the past, a virtual databank of absolutely all past events! The akashic records are located in the spirit world, also known as the astral plane: an invisible layer of infinite space around the Earth and far beyond, welcoming every soul that left the Earth. Only a handful of humans know how to travel to this astral plane and unlock the doors leading to the akashic records. You are one of them! By accessing these records on a virtual screen, one can watch any chosen event from the past! Even one that happened millions of years ago, when the dinosaurs were still roaming the Earth!

This handful of privileged individuals have always been only mere spectators to what they chose to see, without being able to interact with anyone or take part in the past in any way. It is as if they were simply watching a movie projected onto a screen...

...until now...

Faraway, in the country of Nepal, a teenage girl and her twin brother accidentally found a way to penetrate this unique fortress of time, literally entering inside the akashic records' time capsules! In no time, they learned that they had the power to influence the future on Earth by changing its past through the akashic records! They also discovered how to become extremely wealthy by travelling inside this astral plane. Feeling more and more influential, both siblings finally decided that whatever they did not like on Earth...they could alter and eliminate by changing the past. In other words, they would change parts of our planet's history to accommodate their smallest wishes and needs, by completely erasing unwanted past events...even people...

...this is where you come in...

Your mission is to stop these delusional twins from transforming our present world into their own dangerous masquerade. How? No one knows...since no one has ever entered the akashic records' time capsules before. It is something that you will have to figure out on your own...

You have a valuable head start over the siblings: they have no magical powers whatsoever and are not aware of your existence! Use this fact to your advantage.

Best of luck! You are now ready to begin your mission...

ABOUT A SISTER AND HER BROTHER...

In the high mountains of Nepal, a teenage girl called Sunita and her twin brother named Raju were living with their grandmother and grandfather. Both siblings loved each other very much but were condemned to live with a terrible tragedy: the sudden loss of their parents, caused by a deadly avalanche. Since that horrific day, when their parents never came back home, the twins went to live with their caring grandparents, who were martial arts and meditation masters. Guided by them, both Sunita and Raju became experts in those same arts. In addition, they were introduced to and then mastered the art of travelling to the astral plane. Very quickly, both siblings were made aware of the existence of the akashic records. They were then taught how to unlock the gate which led to the past, and this enabled them to watch any piece of history...

Once they found themselves inside the akashic records, Sunita and Raju shared the same thought: to see their parents again. At that moment, they took each other's hands, closed their eyes, and focused on the vivid memories they had of their mother and father. A few seconds later, they found themselves in front of a giant virtual screen which displayed Nepal's breathtaking mountains. As they were staring at the screen, their eyes focused on the bottom of one of those gargantuan peaks. Suddenly, they recognized their parents walking hand-in-hand! Each one was holding a leather pouch filled with fresh food bought at the local market.

"Mom! Dad!" they called out immediately.

But out of nowhere, the rocky ground started to shake as a deafening roar filled the air. Huge boulders started to break from the mountain's highest peaks before rolling down at tremendous speed!

"AVALANCHE!!!" said the father. "RUN KAMALA! RUN!"

Both Kamala and her husband Kundal started to run as fast as they could to find shelter. Quickly realizing they had nowhere to hide, they stopped running...and faced each other...one last time.

"I love you Kamala."

"I love you too Kundal."

As they embraced one another, they were instantaneously buried under an enormous pile of rocks and sand. Just like that, they were gone.

"NOOOOOO!!!" yelled the twins as they watched in horror the appalling scene unravel before their eyes. Both teenagers were suddenly seized by uncontrollable convulsions. Witnessing this horrendous scene woke up extreme feelings of fear, despair, sadness, panic, and anger...Their bodies' molecules started to vibrate at an inconceivable speed, even faster than all the molecules that made up the akashic records! Suddenly, they felt their pulsating bodies sucked inside the time capsule they were witnessing... Immediately, they found themselves right next to the massive pile of rocks and sand which buried their parents: the twins were now part of this time capsule!

"RAJU! WHERE ARE WE?! I THINK WE SOMEHOW ENTERED THIS TIME CAPSULE!"

"I KNOW SISTER, I KNOW! I CAN'T BELIEVE IT TOO! NOW HURRY AND HELP ME!!"

Frantically, Sunita and Raju tried to move the heavy boulders crushing their parents, but the rocks were way too heavy. Crying together, they both fell to their knees as Sunita said:

"I wish we could have warned them about this deadly avalanche."

A few seconds later, the twins felt once again their bodies' molecules vibrate at an incredible speed! Yet again, the siblings were sent back in time into another time capsule...this time, a capsule where their parents had just left the local market, still holding leather pouches.

"WE JUST TRAVELLED BACK IN TIME AGAIN! HOW DID WE DO THAT?" screamed Sunita.

Out of nowhere, a hoarse voice unexpectedly said to them:

"In the spirit world, your bodies are much more susceptible to react to any strong feelings you might have. When you saw your mother and father being buried by the avalanche, you felt a desperate need to try to save them. The atrocious feelings suffocating you were so powerful that it made your bodies' molecules move exceptionally fast in the direction of where you urgently wanted to go. You broke the barrier of time...and are now active participants in time capsules."

The teenage girl and her brother turned around, and saw an older man that looked like some kind of monk. He was dressed in an impeccable white robe, and was levitating a few feet above the ground.

"Who are you?" asked Raju.

Ignoring her brother's question, Sunita slowly approached the man and asked:

"Pardon my ignorance Sir...I am trying to understand your words. Are you saying that in order to travel from one time capsule to another, we simply need to somehow re-experience such horrible feelings again? As if those intense feelings were the fuel which propels us back in time?"

The floating man smiled and said:

"No my dear. Since you have already managed to enter one time capsule, you now can easily enter any time capsule of your choice. The akashic virtual library collects all the time capsules of the past. You can simply visualize where you want to be, and what you want to see in order to enter any time capsule. But beware: entering a time capsule must be used only for the good of mankind. Remember that by altering a past event or outcome, you impact everything and everyone around you..."

"Who are you, old man?" yaps Raju.

The man dressed in white frowned at the teenager's audacity and rudeness, and simply disappeared. Raju quickly stood up, and glanced at his twin sister before telling her:

"I know exactly what we are going to do. Follow me sister..."

MAGICAL SKILLS

During the long and tough nine years you spent in Tibet, you learned many magical skills from the High Priest. Now is the time for you to choose five magical skills that are going to be yours throughout this mission. Choose wisely because once you start your quest, you will not be allowed to change the magical skills you have picked...

1. **Telepathy:** This skill allows you to read people's thoughts and to send them messages with your mind.

2. **Telekinesis:** This skill enables you to quickly move almost any object or person from one spot to another with the power of your mind; you can do so from any distance.

3. **Invisibility:** Becoming invisible at will and in any circumstances can be a real life-saver, especially when you find yourself in front of many dangerous enemies.

4. **Flying:** Mastering this skill allows you to fly like a bird at any height and any speed you want, even at the speed of mind!

5. **Sixth Sense:** This skill enables you to feel what is the best course of action to take in a given situation, including which way to go when you are on the road. It allows you to feel the presence of your enemies and of any other danger.

6. **Owl's Eyes:** This skill allows you to see as clearly during the night (or in any dark place) as you do during the day, just like an owl!

7. **Heavenly Shield:** This is the ultimate shield of protection; nothing can get through it. By mastering this skill, you can make this shield appear on your forearm at any time and block whatever projectile comes your way.

8. **Eternal Breath:** Mastering this skill means being able to breathe under water for an unlimited period of time.

9. **Fire Jet:** This skill allows you to throw blazing fire jets with amazing precision and power through short and long distances.

10. **Paralysis:** With this skill, you can touch or strike any opponents' vital points and paralyze them from head to toe. You can also knock an enemy unconscious with a single finger pressure.

11. **Ice Bolts:** This skill enables you to throw huge bolts of ice with great precision and strength through long and short distances. When the ice bolt comes into contact with its target, that target becomes completely frozen.

12. **Iron Bolt:** With this skill, you can throw big bolts of iron on a specific target. It is ideal for blasting a heavy door, a very thick wall, or even gigantic artificial life forms.

13. **Laser Eyes:** This skill allows you to send a powerful red laser beam with your eyes! It is excellent for melting almost anything, including metal and rocks!!

14. **Tornado:** This amazing skill is introduced for the first time in the DETERMINE YOUR DESTINY series. Simply imagine yourself spinning so fast that you metamorphose yourself into a powerful tornado! That's what this skill allows you to do...and so much more!

YOUR MAGICAL SKILLS

PUT A CHECK MARK NEXT TO THE POWERS YOU CHOOSE

1. Telepathy ☐

2. Telekinesis ☐

3. Invisibility ☐

4. Flying ☐

5. Sixth Sense ☐

6. Owl's Eyes ☐

7. Heavenly Shield ☐

8. Eternal Breath ☐

9. Fire Jet ☐

10. Paralysis ☐

11. Ice Bolt ☐

12. Laser Eyes ☐

13. Iron Bolt ☐

14. Tornado ☐

1

The evening sky is clear and tainted with a reddish aura from the bright sun about to hide in the faraway horizon. A delicious smell of fresh grilled chicken, coming from your neighbour's backyard, delicately fills the air as you pleasantly converse with your special guests. Comfortably sitting on the beautifully crafted pine wood patio chairs, the High Priest of Tibet and his sister, the High Priestess, are enjoying a warm cup of butter tea in your company. Just before their arrival, you also prepared a succulent homemade tsampa. It's a Tibetan cereal made with roasted barely, resembling corn cereal.

"This is really delicious, *Chosen One*," says the High Priestess.

"I'm so glad you like it," you answer with a smile.

"You did not forget how to prepare our Tibetan cuisine," continues the older wise woman. "I am impressed."

"How could I forget?"

After a short moment of silence, the High Priest takes another sip of your delicious tea, looks at you, and says:

"*Chosen One*, once again I must emphasize how truly sorry we are. We don't know how to help you in your quest to stop the Nepalese twins Sunita and Raju, since we have no idea on how to enter the akashic records' time capsules."

"You will find a way, *Chosen One*. You always have and you always will. We believe in you."

"Thank you, High Priestess. Your trust in me means everything. I don't know how but I will find a way to enter those time capsules. If the Nepalese twins did it, so can I. Until then, may I offer you two some more tea and tsampa?"

"Yes please," replies the High Priest. "It is truly delectable!"

"Simply scrumptious," continues further his sister.

For the rest of the evening, you chat with your friends about what is currently happening in your lives, remembering what you have all been through together in the past. You look at your exceptional friends and think that surviving the plane crash above Tibet was for you a blessing in disguise. If it wasn't for their help, wisdom and care, you would not be alive today...

"Well sister," says the High Priest, "I believe it is time for us to return to our monastery in Tibet."

"My dear brother, you once again beat me to it. I was just about to say that. The *Chosen One*'s mission starts tomorrow morning, so a proper rest is a must."

You all get up, and approach one another to say 'goodbye'.

"*Chosen One*," says the wise man, "you have always excelled at helping people. Your heart is pure, and your skills are unmatched. We have no doubt that you can once again succeed in your mission, no matter how difficult it appears to be now."

His sister takes your hands, and looks deeply into your eyes:

"Do what you do best *Chosen One*: follow your amazing instincts, use your unique magical skills when needed, and listen to your heart. Our spirits will always be with you."

"Thank you both for such encouraging words, and for paying me such a wonderful visit tonight. We will have many more pleasurable evenings like tonight, I promise."

"We know *Chosen One*," say your mentors gratefully in unison.

"Stay safe...and come back soon," adds the High Priestess.

"I will my friends."

Both of your guests delicately reach out to you, and gently touch your forehead with the tips of their fingers. A warm green light appears on your skin upon contact with their fingertips. Slowly, both brother and sister disappear before your eyes, sending you a beautiful smile. Now standing alone in your backyard, you look up towards the sky, thinking:

"I must accomplish my mission. I have to."

You quickly clean up all the dishes, and prepare yourself to go to bed. Your mind is racing, and you can't stop thinking about how you will enter the akashic records' time capsules. As soon as your head hits your pillow, you receive a telepathic message from the High Priest:

"You will be fine, Chosen One. Life has always been on your side."

You close your eyes, relax your body, and a few minutes later...you are fast asleep.

Have a good night...and wake up at section 7

2

"As I said before, my name is Gutuk. I am the gate keeper of time. For thousands of years, I have had the privilege to learn everything there is to know about the akashic records and their time capsules."

"So you have lived in the spirit world for thousands of years?"

"That is correct, *Chosen One*. From the spirit world, I was always aware of everything that was happening on Earth, since the beginning of time. That is how I know who you are, and why you are here. For instance, I know your heart is pure, and you want to stop the Nepalese twins: Sunita and her brother Raju."

"Yes I do. What can you tell me about these twins?"

Continue your journey to section 9

3

"I think I'm ready to enter a time capsule," you tell Gutuk.

"Hmm... you do not seem convinced," replies the older man.

"I mean...it sounds nerve-racking...but I think I'm ready."

"This will be a very intense experience, *Chosen One*. You do not have to go through this process now if you are not sure if you are ready."

Suddenly, Gutuk receives a telepathic message from an old acquaintance. He closes his eyes, focusing on the words that he is hearing. A moment later, he looks at you and says:

"I just received an urgent message from a long-time friend. She lives in Kathmandu with her granddaughter Shirisha. She's asking me to quickly verify an important detail for her from the akashic records. I am sorry *Chosen One* but our adventure into a time capsule will have to wait.

Continue your journey to section 8

4

Your extremely well-developed sixth sense tells you that you can trust Gutuk with your life! You strongly feel that your encounter with this pleasant man has a very deep purpose...

It's time for section 2

5

"As the gate keeper of time, I have the authority to reset all time capsules to their original state. In other words, if Sunita and her brother alter the past in any way to change the future on Earth, I have the right to undo the changes they have done. This way, everything on Earth would go back to the way it was before any given time capsule alteration. I can also block the twins' access to any time capsule."

"So why don't you do it now?" you ask perplexed.

"I may have the authority, but I don't have enough power and might in me. My spirit is strong but their spirits, combined together, are stronger. This is where I need your help. If you bring the twins to me, I will be able to eliminate all changes they have made to any moment in time, and block them forever from entering ANY time capsule."

"Then...I must bring them back to you, Gutuk!"

"Thank you, *Chosen One.* Once the twins will be facing me, we will have to act very quickly in order not to give them the chance to escape into another time capsule. A few seconds is all they would need to escape, by simply imagining where they want to go," explains the old man.

"So what is your plan?"

"When you arrive in the spirit world with Raju and Sunita, I will place my hand on your forehead to join my spirit with yours, while you touch their heads. The strength you have in you will increase mine, and I will only then be able to remedy the situation once and for all."

"Understood. Where do I start?"

"I can tell you right now that for several reasons, you will eventually have to enter a time capsule during your mission. As soon as you do, you will then be able to enter any time capsule of your choice, and at any time. You can try now if you think you are ready. If not, you can go back to your house on Earth, and start getting ready to leave for Nepal. Since the twins are often supervising the construction of their palace, you have a very good chance of finding them in Kang Guru Mountain.

If you wish to immediately enter a time capsule to start travelling back in time, enter section 3!

If you want to go back home, fly away to section 8

6

You smile at the two well-dressed men as you say:

"Gentlemen, there is a parking ticket booth right here...to the left of the airport's entrance."

You take a few steps towards the booth. You immediately hear a very loud metallic noise above your head. You look up and see an enormous metallic beam falling from the sky towards you. It's about to smash onto the ground, right where you are standing! In order to avoid being hit by the deadly beam, you barely have time to jump to the side. As it hits the ground, attached to it, you notice two large rusty broken cables.

"Nice reflex," says the shorter man. "Are you alright?"

"I'm fine, thank you."

"One can never be too careful around here with all this construction," he continues. "By the way, would you happen to have some spare change? We have to pay our parking fare at the booth, and we just realized we don't have any money."

"You don't need change," you answer the shorter man. "You can use your credit card."

"We both left our wallets at my place this morning. We feel so silly. Could you please help us and let us use yours? It would only be around twenty dollars."

"Sorry guys. I don't carry change nor a credit card."

Obviously irritated by your composure, the taller of the two men quickly approaches you and says:

"Enough of this nonsense. Give us your backpack, and you won't get hurt."

"I don't think so," you briskly answer, "but I will gladly show you a few of my...tricks. Are you ready?"

"Are you some kind of magician?" asks the shorter man.

"Something like that," you reply.

"Enough!" says the tall man as he pulls out a short knife.

If you have the skill of telepathy, walk to section 11

If you master the skill of telekinesis, go to section 21

If you know how to become invisible, disappear at section 17

If you mastered shooting lasers with your eyes, shoot some at section 14

If you have the ice bolt skill, prepare yourself for section 18

If you are a fire jet master, get ready for section 16

If you prefer using your martial arts expertise, to do at section 20

7

You wake up the following morning feeling well-rested, energized but very nervous. You literally jump out of bed, and quickly freshen up before getting dressed. You walk to the kitchen to prepare yourself a solid breakfast like you always do...but this time you stop in front of your large rectangular kitchen window, staring at the big trees climbing into the sky from your backyard.

"I don't feel hungry," you tell yourself, *"but I must eat at least a little something. This mission is making me more nervous that I taught."*

You grab a homemade blueberry muffin from your fridge, and make yourself a mouth-watering cup of hot coco. You slowly eat while sipping your hot beverage, still staring through the window.

"I must do this..."

You finish eating, and walk to your bright living room. With your tough mission invading your mind, you sit on your superb leather couch before lying on your back.

"I know that I have visited the akashic records before, but I have never entered a time capsule. I would have never thought that entering one was a possibility. All right...here I go...let's see where my journey takes me..."

You close your eyes, breathing very deeply and slowly. You visualize your body becoming lighter and lighter, focusing on the infinite energy flowing through your body. You start accelerating the movement of your body's molecules. Within seconds your molecules are moving so fast that your body becomes transparent...and finally disappears. You feel your entire being fly higher and higher, as you enter a monumental tunnel of luminous white light. Your body is propelled forward at tremendous speed as you reach the lustrous spirit world. In your mind, you see the limitless field where you need to be, a field that is constantly surrounded by the brightest light which never hurts the eyes. A moment later, you are standing in the middle of that grandiose field: the akashic records themselves!

"Once again I am here in the akashic records. What am I supposed to do now? How do I actually get inside a time capsule?"

You place your hands in front of you as if you were touching a glass window. Immediately, a light blue virtual screen the size of a house appears in front of you! You take a moment to study the imposing screen. Since you already know what triggers the images to be displayed on the screen, you think to yourself:

"I wish to see myself last night in the company of the High Priestess and her brother."

Instantly, a crystal clear image appears on the superb screen: your life-long mentor, the High Priest, and yourself eating fresh homemade tsampa, and drinking steamy butter tea.

Observing the screen, you ask yourself the simple question: *"How am I supposed to get inside a time capsule? "*

For the first time ever, you unexpectedly hear a very pleasant voice nearby.

"May I be of service, *Chosen One?*"

You look around you, and right away notice an older man nearby, smiling at you. He looks like a monk, is dressed in an immaculate white robe, and is floating a few feet above the ground.

"My name is Gutuk," he says. "I have been expecting you..."

If you want to ask for his help, prepare yourself for section 2

If you decline his help, get ready for section 12

If you master the sixth sense, float to section 4

8

"I must go back to the human world, and then travel to Nepal," you tell Gutuk. "I need to stop Raju and Sunita as soon as possible. When the time comes, I will come back to the spirit world and with your help, I will enter a time capsule!"

"Very well," replies the old wise man. "I wish you a safe trip to Kang Guru Mountain, and remember that I will do everything I can to help you in your mission. Go in peace, *Chosen One.*"

"Thank you Gutuk."

You close your eyes, and immediately feel your body's molecules starting to vibrate faster and faster. You feel as your body is lifted up by a gentle force, higher and higher. Before you know it, you are back in the tunnel of marvelous white light, flying at a remarkable speed, and feeling as if a warm invisible blanket is wrapping itself all around you. A short moment later, you open your eyes, and find yourself back in your living room. You feel your comfortable plush leather couch under your relaxed body. You get up, and give your whole body a good stretch.

"Time to pack and leave for Nepal," you tell yourself.

You walk to your bedroom, take out your backpack, and start filling it with everything you need. In no time, you are packed and ready to go. You pick up the phone, and call for a taxi.

Wait for the taxi at section 15

9

Gutuk moves closer towards you and says:

"Deep down inside, Sunita has a good heart, but she is very much influenced by her brother. Raju is very selfish, rude, arrogant, and believes he deserves to have everything he wants. He does not care if his decisions make others suffer, and is also a master at convincing his sister to follow in his footsteps."

"What damage have they done at this point?"

"Since they discovered how to enter a time capsule, their focus has been on becoming wealthy...very wealthy! Due to the molecular similarities between the Earth and the spirit world, it is possible to bring back any object from a time capsule to Earth."

"Incredible!" you say in astonishment.

"So far, the twins have travelled back in time to many places, and managed to gather a great deal of wealth. For instance, they entered a time capsule last week to find themselves on a Spanish Empire ship sailing on the Pacific Ocean hundreds of years ago. That particular vessel was carrying an unbelievably large treasure made of gold coins, precious stones, jewels, silver, and more. As experts in martial arts, Sunita and Raju easily neutralized the soldiers guarding the treasure, and quickly stole it! In the last few days, they also entered another time capsule to find themselves inside an Egyptian pyramid filled with all kinds of ancient tomb treasures. Once again, they stole everything of value."

"What do they need all these treasures for?" you inquire.

"They want them in order to finance, and furnish a sumptuous palace that is being built for them as we speak, in the Nepalese Kang Guru

Mountain," replies Gutuk. "They specifically chose that mountain because they believe it will bring them good fortune! They also wish to expand their territory."

"What do you mean?"

"They want more and more land for themselves because of its phenomenal value. They are also ready to recruit and pay a vast army of soldiers who will be devoted to them. Raju secretly wants his own army to take over the Nepalese government."

"So he is ready to instigate a civil war," you sadly say, imagining the horrific scene.

"Yes he is. Also, as the High Priest of Tibet already told you, both siblings - especially Raju - have decided that whatever events they did not like on Earth today, they would eliminate by changing the past."

"Have they started such abominable deeds?"

"Not yet," replies Gutuk. "They are too busy enjoying their preposterous wealth, and monitoring how their excessive palace is being built!"

"How can I stop them?" you ask the older man.

"You could try to somehow capture them once they are inside a time capsule, and then bring them to me, or you can try to neutralize them on Earth, and then bring them to me."

"But how can I bring them to you? I have never travelled with anyone into or within the spirit world."

"In time, you will find out," reassures you Gutuk.

"And then what?"

"Then, it is I that will need your help," says the older man with a very serious face.

Get ready for section 5

10

Your fabulous sixth sense warns you that these two men are crooks, and will try to rob you! On top of that, you feel an imminent danger coming your way, threatening your life...

**If you want to show the parking ticket booth to the two young men
and quickly walk away, pass by section 6**

If you prefer to simply say, 'No,' walk to section 13

If you prefer to completely ignore these men, do so at section 19

11

You stare at both men in front of you, activating your superb telepathic ability. Without any warning, you send them both the same powerful brain wave which strongly resonates inside their heads:

"WALK AWAY NOW BEFORE YOU REGRET IT! I AM IN TOTAL CONTROL OF WHAT YOU HEAR. BE VERY CAREFUL OR I WILL ZAP YOUR BRAINS WITH AN ELECTRIC CURRENT!"

Both crooks gawk at you in disbelief, and take a few steps back before running away from you towards the parking lot. As if nothing had happened, you resume walking before going through the airport's main entrance.

Continue your journey at section 25

12

"I think I can manage on my own, but I appreciate your offer," you kindly reply.

"As you wish," says Gutuk.

He becomes transparent, and disappears, leaving you with a sense of discomfort, loneliness, and incertitude. Once again you look at the massive screen in front of you, contemplating the crystal clear image of you and your devoted friends greatly enjoying themselves last night. You touch the thin screen...but your hand goes right through it. You decide to try to jump into it, but your body goes through, and you land on the other side of the screen.

"How am I supposed to do this?" you says in frustration.

You sit down, and think: *"Touching the screen doesn't do anything; jumping inside the screen only makes me get on its other side...I don't know anymore! I think I actually do need help..."*

"There is nothing wrong with admitting that one needs help," says a familiar voice above you. You lift your head up, and notice Gutuk. "May I now be of instance?" he says genuinely.

"Yes please. I do need your help more than ever. Forgive me for refusing it earlier."

Get up in section 2

13

"Sorry gentlemen, I don't know," you simply answer as you continue walking.

"Wait!" says the shorter of the two men. "This fell out of your backpack."

He walks up to you, followed by his buddy, and hands you a blue pen.

"This isn't mine," you answer the short man.

Without any warning, he immediately pushes you to the ground. You fall onto your backpack, and instantly hear a very loud metallic noise resonate above your head. You look up and see a gigantic metal beam falling straight at you...but it's too late for you to get out of the way...

...a moment ago, two cables holding the enormous metallic beam abruptly snapped, which caused the beam to fall directly on you! You failed your mission before it even started! It is so sad that such a random accident took your life...just like that...

...or was it an accident? You will never know.

THE END

14

"Pulling a knife on people is never a good idea," you tell the man.

You focus on the blade turned towards you, and unexpectedly, you shoot two bright red laser beams out of your eyes. One of them hits the blade while the other one hits the hooligan's hand.

"Aaaaaaah!" screams the crook as he drops the knife.

"No way!" says his accomplice. "How is that possible?!"

"Who cares? Let's get out of here!!"

Both thieves run away towards the cars in the parking lot. You walk towards the airport's entrance as if nothing had happened...with a smile on your face.

Enter the airport at section 25

15

Fifteen minutes later, a taxi stops in front of your house where you are already waiting. You open the back door and sit on the back seat, putting your backpack next to you. You immediately recognize the driver: a very nice older lady named Nana who drove you many times before:

"Good afternoon, Nana. How are you this morning?"

"I am feeling great, thank you! Before picking you up, I just made myself a freshly squeezed orange juice. It was so refreshing! So...where are you going today?"

"I am going to the airport."

"Of course," replies Nana. "Off we go!"

The car slowly drives away towards the airport as you look through the window, wondering what the future holds for you. You exchange a few words with Nana, mostly listening to her talking about her grandchildren, and imminent retirement. About half an hour later, you arrive at the airport.

"Thank you for the ride Nana."

"It's always a pleasure, dear. You have a nice trip, and watch out for the construction outside the airport. They are renovating the whole place!"

You pay your fare, grab your backpack, and are about to walk inside the airport when two young men approach you on your right. Both individuals are wearing well-tailored expensive looking

suits with white shirts and black ties.

"Excuse us," says the tallest man, "would you happen to know where we can pay for parking?"

At the same time, you notice a parking ticket booth to the left of the airport's entrance.

**If you want to show the parking ticket booth to the two men,
be helpful at section 6**

If you prefer to simply say 'no', walk to section 13

If you master the sixth sense, go to section 10

If you prefer to completely ignore these men, do so at section 19

16

"I would not do this if I were you," you tell the tall thief while opening a wave of magic inside your being. "Put your knife down and walk away...or else..."

"Are you threatening me?" asks the arrogant crook.

"I am not the one holding the knife," you reply.

Swiftly, you throw a thin fire jet on the weapon's handle, partially hitting his hand.

"Aaaaaaaaah!" screams the tall crook. You immediately throw a few more fire jets at their feet, hitting their shoes. Petrified and dumbfounded, the two crooks run away from you as fast as they possibly can, in the opposite direction that they came from. Taking your time, you turn around, and finally walk inside the airport.

Prepare yourself for section 25

17

You quickly look around you, and see no other people in sight who might witness what you are about to do.

"Goodbye gentlemen," you simply say.

Slowly, your body starts to become transparent. A moment later, you completely disappear and become invisible to the thieves, even if you are still standing in the same spot!

"Incredible!" says the shorter man.

Suddenly, you deliver a powerful front kick to the tall man's hand holding the short knife. The weapon is catapulted far away, ending up inside a garbage can. Holding his sore hand and in panic mode, the crook says:

"Let's get out of this crazy place!"

Both men start running towards the cars in the nearby parking lot. A moment later, you choose to reappear inside the airport, after sneaking inside one of its washrooms.

"*This way, no one saw me reappear,*" you tell yourself as you walk out of the empty washroom.

Take a walk to section 25

18

While focusing on the hand holding the weapon, a huge flow of magic emerges from inside you. You quickly feel the ice coming to the surface of your hands, gently tickling them. Faster than lightening, you throw an ice bolt the size of a watermelon at the knife! It instantaneously freezes the weapon as well at the hand holding it. The two crooks look at you as if you were a supernatural being, not believing what just happened. Out of the blue, you then throw a fantastic hammer kick onto the ice bolt, pulverizing it into a thousand tiny pieces. Speechless and scared for their lives, the thieves run away towards the parking lot.

"*That will teach them*", you tell yourself.

A moment later, you walk inside the airport.

Continue your mission to section 25

19

You look at these two well-dressed men, but prefer to simply walk towards the airport entrance. With all the renovations going on around you, you suddenly hear a very loud metallic noise resonate above your head. You look up...but it's too late. Two cables holding an enormous metallic beam abruptly snap, causing the beam to fall directly to the ground...but crushing you first! You perish instantaneously, not feeling a thing. Your mission is sadly over...but so is the future of the world.

What a crazy accident...

...or was it?

THE END

20

In an unbelievably fast movement, you grab the hand holding the knife, and deliver a powerful right hook to the thug's jaw. The tall man crumbles to the ground, now knocked out. Before he can realize what is happening, the second thief receives an extraordinary spinning heel kick to the stomach. He has nowhere to go but down, completely out of breath. You quickly call airport security, and in no time, the crooks are in their custody.

"Good job," says a female officer. "How did you manage to defend yourself in such a situation?"

"I got lucky," you simply answer. "Thank you for your help."

You turn around, and walk inside the airport.

Let's go to section 25

21

You feel your astonishing magical powers waking up inside you, as you stare at the tall man holding the short knife. Slowly, as you raise your right hand up in the air, you lift the armed man a few feet off the ground at the same time! Seized with panic, he starts to wiggle in the air like a fish out of water.

"What is happening to me? How are you doing this? STOP! PUT ME DOWN!"

"Then throw your knife to the ground right now," you tell him seriously.

He immediately complies to your demand. As you lower your hand down, he automatically drops to the ground at the same time. Both men immediately start running away from you towards the parking lot.

You watch them escape for a moment, and calmly resume walking before going through the airport's main entrance.

It is time for section 25

22

The flight is very long but comfortable. Thanks to a fluffy pillow, you are able to get some decent sleep, and to rest. You find the food delicious, and the service excellent. On top of that, you are able to watch your favorite television shows on a small screen mounted in the seat in front of you. Hours later, your plane lands in Kathmandu, the capital of Nepal.

"Ladies and gentlemen, this is your captain speaking. We have arrived at Tribhuvan International Airport in Kathmandu, Nepal. It is now 8:00pm local time. On behalf of myself and the entire crew, thank you for flying with us, and enjoy your stay in Nepal."

A few minutes later, you grab your backpack, and follow the other passengers off the plane, and into the large airport. After going through customs, you reach the airport's exit.

"Even though I slept on the plane, I still feel my body needs to stretch and rest on a comfortable bed. It's getting late anyway. I will take a taxi to one of the nicer hotels I read about in my travel guide. It's a good thing that many people speak English here."

You walk up to a taxi, and start speaking with driver. He is an older man with a big belly, a great smile, and a pleasant sense of humour.

"Good evening Sir."

"Good evening. My name is Ram. It rhymes with ham."

"Nice to meet you Ram. Can you please take me to the Yak and Yeti Hotel in Kathmandu?"

"Of course. Please come in."

"How far is it?"

"It is quite close."

You sit in the back with your backpack next to you, and let your eyes roam around the city before you, as the cab drives away into the night.

Enjoy the view all the way to section 30

23

You notice two colossal men standing behind all the others. With the amazing power of your mind, you choose to slightly lift the two brutes off the ground, before throwing them with force onto the other men. They all fall down like bowling pins, confused and in pain. The chubby man is the first one to get up. With the invisible force of your mind, you push him abruptly onto three other guys. You choose to repeat this scenario a few times until the men, bruised up, start to run in the opposite direction, leaving you and the young couple behind.

Now relax in section 31

24

All the men pick up a rock from the side of the road, and walk towards you with a smirk on their faces.

"You want to throw rocks at me? That's not very nice. Actually, I too am very good at this game."

With very fast movements, you throw an ice bolt at each one of the men's torsos. You do so with such force, and agility that each bolt crashes upon impact, breaking into thousands of pieces.

"Aaaaaaaaaah!!" scream the men in pain. "Aaaaaaaaah! RUN AWAY FROM THE CRAZY FAKIR!"

"*I think they got my message,*" you tell yourself.

Turn around to section 31

25

"*Those guys got what they deserved,*" you tell yourself as you walk inside the airport. You go straight to a nearby ticket office.

"Good morning," says a pleasant young woman at the ticket booth. "May I help you?"

"Certainly. I would like to buy a round trip ticket to Kathmandu, in Nepal."

"Very well," answers the employee. "If you also wish to purchase Nepalese rupees, you will find a currency exchange office behind me."

"Thank you. I will definitely need to purchase some."

After buying your plane ticket to Kathmandu, the young woman says:

"Your flight will depart in two hours from gate number five. I wish you a pleasant flight."

"Thank you very much."

You go to the currency exchange office, and buy a large quantity of Nepalese rupees. You count your money before putting it safely away, and start walking towards one of the many security gates...

After walking through a metal detector, and showing your passport to a security staff, you throw your backpack on one shoulder before continuing to walk towards gate number five. You glance at all the restaurants and duty-free stores, and decide to stop in a little shop to buy a book entitled *Travel Guide to Nepal*. You then find gate five, and sit in a comfortable chair before looking at your watch.

"*I have about 90 minutes before boarding the plane.*"

You take out your book, and start reading it. You find Nepal's geography fascinating with all its great mountains like Everest, Kanchenjungu, Lhotse, Makalu, and many more.

"*Wow! All those mountains are the highest in the world!*"

You let your eyes roam through the book, and discover more information regarding the country's economy, political system, language, culture, education system, and currency. Before you know it, you hear the following announcement:

"All passengers flying to Kathmandu, Nepal, are being requested for boarding at gate number five."

You immediately present yourself to the gate with your boarding pass, and your passport. After looking at it, the airport employee says: "Thank you. Enjoy your flight."

A moment later, you are sitting inside the plane by the window, reading your book about Nepal.

"*This is really interesting...*"

Shortly after boarding, the aircraft leaves gate number five. A few minutes later, its powerful engines propel the plane towards a mysterious country, full of beauty and grace...a country now in serious jeopardy because of an evil brother and his sister...

Keep flying to section 22

26

You focus on the entire group of men getting closer to you, activating your unmatched telepathic ability. You hastily send them a very strong brain wave which resonates like massive bells inside their head:

"STOP THE ABUSE! NO MORE!! LEAVE NOW OR YOU WILL SEE WHAT WILL HAPPEN TO YOU!!!"

The men abruptly grab their heads with both hands, panic now bulging out of their eyes. They all look at you as if you were a powerful magician of some sort, and frantically start running away.

Walk to section 31

27

"We warned you," says the bald man.

He throws his chubby fist towards your face but you easily deflect the punch, and strike him back with two fingers to the sternum. The man's face becomes white as he collapses onto the filthy ground, physically paralyzed.

Immediately, you jump high into the air, and land in the middle, amongst of the remaining six men. You literally explode with a series of incredibly powerful strikes to their bodies. One after the other, the men drop like flies. A moment later, all your opponents are down, physically unable to move, and in bad shape. You have paralyzed them!

Now it's time for section 31

28

All seven men pick up whatever object they can find on the ground, and begin to approach you. The short chubby man suddenly throws a piece of brick at you, but you pulverize it in mid-air with a roundhouse kick!

"*Enough of this*," you tell yourself.

You jump into the air towards the men, sending each foot in the opposite direction while executing a split. Each foot smashes into each man's face, sending them both to the ground. You immediately turn around, and explode with a powerful combination of punches and kicks, sending down three more men. Unexpectedly, the two men still left standing grab your arms and try to stop you, but you know better...You easily smash them to the hard ground using a classic Tibetan throw.

"I can't believe my eyes," says the young woman behind you, holding onto her husband.

Go talk to them at section 31

29

You let yourself get surrounded by the seven men, now looking at you with a smirk. You notice that some of the men reach for large chunks of brick lying on the ground in the rubble surrounding them.

"I am giving all of you the chance to walk away, and avoid getting hurt," you announce.

They all start laughing at you, curious to see what you are about to do.

"As you wish," you simply say.

Immediately activating your inner magical flow, you start spinning extremely fast in the spot where you are standing. You open your arms to further expend what you are becoming...You are now spinning so fast that you suddenly become invisible, creating all around your body an extremely powerful whirlwind...finally turning yourself into a tornado!

You rapidly move towards the panicked men who are now trying to escape but cannot. You touch the chubby man with your whirlwind, and he is catapulted far away into thick bushes!

"NOOOO...PLEASE DON'T HURT US!" beg the men. "PLEASE!!"

Slowly, you stop spinning, and are back to your normal self. You look at the remaining six men, and say:

"If I hear that you are still harming this couple or anyone else for that matter, I will find you all, and we will have a little chat. Am I clear?"

"YES! YES! VERY CLEAR!" answer the men unanimously.

"Now leave," you order them.

All men start running away, petrified yet still not believing what just happened to them.

It is time to go to section 31

30

"I think the outskirts of Kathmandu are very interesting," you tell Ram. "The homes are nicely decorated, the people seem friendly, the many shops I see carry a variety of appealing products..."

"Some people are happy, some others are not. We just survived an earthquake two weeks ago. It was very devastating. The aftermath still affects many."

"I am sorry to hear that."

A few minutes later, Ram looks at you in his rear-view mirror, and says:

"We are now driving through a poor neighborhood very much affected by the earthquake. You will not like it."

Through the window, your eyes see destroyed homes, wrecked gardens, crumbled buildings, ripped off roofs, broken fences, people sleeping in open tents under plastic bags...

"This is horrible! Is the Nepalese government helping these poor people?" you ask Ram.

"Yes but the government can only do so much. There is not enough money to rebuild everything and help everyone."

"How sad and unfortunate..."

Your eyes abruptly stop on a revolting scene unveiling on the right side of the road: a young couple are surrounded by a group of seven aggressive men. The brutes appear to be intimidating, and are pushing the couple

around. The young woman and the man look very scared and defenseless.

"RAM! STOP THE CAR!"

"I don't think..."

"SLAM THE BRAKES!"

The taxi immediately comes to a halt next to the group, as you jump out of the car, yelling:

"HEY! LEAVE THEM ALONE!!!"

Everyone turns around to look at you, obviously surprised by your hasty appearance.

"GO HOME AND LEAVE THIS COUPLE ALONE AT ONCE!

Ignoring the young couple for a moment, the group of men slowly walk up to you. A chubby little man with a bald head dares to address you:

"This is not your problem. Mind your own business."

"When I see such injustice and abuse, I make it my business!" you reply.

"If you don't leave now, you will regret it," says another.

"I am not leaving," you continue. "BUT YOU ALL WILL!"

If you are a tornado master, get ready for section 29

If you master the skill of paralysis, it's time to use it in section 27

If you have the skill of telekinesis, clean up the mess in section 23

If you are a telepathy master, get ready for section 26

If you bear the ice bolt skill, cool off these men in section 24

If you don't have any the above skills or simply prefer to use your martial art expertise, jump straight into section 28

31

You approach the young pair. The couple stare at you as if you were their guardian angel.

"We can't thank you enough for defending us against those men. You saved my wife's...I mean our lives!" says the husband.

"It was the least I could do," you kindly reply.

"What you did was truly magical! Are you some kind of fakir with special abilities?" asks the wife.

"You mean some kind of sorcerer?" you ask the lady.

"Yes," she answers.

"I guess you could say that. Why were these men after you?"

"After the earthquake," continues the young woman, "many people did not have enough food to eat. Where we live, the earthquake did not affect us that much. We are very fortunate to still have a home in one piece, and fresh food from our garden. Tonight, we brought some goods to my parents. They insist on staying in this neighborhood in order to slowly rebuild their home. Some of their neighbours saw us, and got angry with us for not bringing them any food. So they went after us...until you showed up!"

"I think you two must come up with a better solution where you can still help your parents, without jeopardizing your safety. What happened today could have been much worse for you."

"You are right," replies the husband.

"How will you get home tonight?"

"We have a car," says the woman.

"Good. Go home and stay safe."

"Thank you once again!" says the couple.

"My pleasure." You get back into the taxi and tell Ram: "We can go now."

Looking at you with great admiration, the older man smiles, and drives away. A minute later, he tells you:

"What you did for those people was incredibly brave! They will remember it for the rest of their lives. I did not know that some fakirs have such unique powers! Well done!!"

"I am always glad to help," you humbly reply.

Drive away to section 36

32

You walk inside the sumptuous hotel, taking a good look around you. The shiny floor is made of large wooden mosaic tiles on which many tall exotic plants are placed, delicately perfuming the air. The thick walls are freshly painted, and decorated with wood carvings which ornate the very tall ceiling. On both sides of the main lobby, a set of grand stairs leads to the upper floors.

You reach the main desk and speak to a lady with the name *Aliya* written on her name tag:

"Good evening. I don't have a reservation, but I would like a room for the night."

"Certainly," answers the hotel employee. "I have a room available on the first floor next to the dining area. Room number twenty-four."

"That will be perfect."

You pay for you room up front, and receive the key to it. Aliya tells you:

"Breakfast will be served tomorrow morning from 7:00am to 11:00am. If you wish to have a meal tonight, the kitchen will be open until 11:00pm. You will find room twenty-four at the end of the hallway to your right. Enjoy your stay."

"Thank you very much."

You quickly reach the end of the hallway, and find your room. You enter it, and find a stunning room with bright walls covered with impressive large laminated pictures of Nepal's most famous architectural designs. The bathroom has been covered with pretty white porcelain tiles everywhere, and your king size bed reminds you how tired your body feels after such a long flight.

"*First, I need to satisfy my hungry stomach.*"

You leave your backpack on the large and comfortable bed, take some rupees with you, and leave your room. You find the opulent dining area on your right, and take a seat at a magnificently set table. Immediately, a waiter comes to you with a menu.

"Good evening. My name is Bishal, and I will be your waiter tonight." He hands you a menu. "Our special for tonight is the dal soup followed by our unique momo plate."

"What is the dal soup made with?" you ask.

"It is made with lentils, and various spices. The momo plate represents an assortment of fresh dumplings, filled will pork that has been delicately seasoned with spices. Is is served with a yellow sesame sauce, as well as a red garlic chili sauce. It is a little spicy but sweet."

"It all sounds delicious. I will have what you suggested."

The waiter takes your menu, pores you some water, smiles, and walks away. You look around the room, and see a few people enjoying a fancy meal. Sitting to your left, two elegantly-dressed men are talking while drinking chiya's tea. One man is wearing a blue suit, and the other is wearing a black tuxedo. You accidently hear the man in the blue suit say:

"Listen Kiran, I don't like what those two teenagers are doing. I don't know where they got their fortune from, but they are filthy rich!"

"They sure are, Manish. Thanks to all the money they have, they just bought a very expensive special permit to build that silly palace at the bottom of Kang Guru. What for?"

"I am not sure, but a legend says that Kang Guru mountain brings great fortune to those that are in direct contact with it."

"And you believe such nonsense Kiran?"

"Of course not. I'm just worried about what's going to happen next. Money always leads to some kind of power. Next thing you know, they will try to buy out our government to fulfill their selfish needs. "

After hearing these words, you realize who the two men are talking about. Sunita and Raju are moving fast, and time is definitively not on your side. Out of nowhere, an old lady appears on the chair in front of you! She is dressed in a traditional folkloric Nepalese dress, and her silky white hair is tied in a bun at the top of her head. She stares at you with great interest, and smiles.

"Hello, *Chosen One*. My name is Manna. I will not take much of your time but we need to talk. Your food will not be ready for at least another 20 minutes, which gives us enough time. Do you want to stay here or prefer to go to your room to speak in private?"

If you wish to remain in the dining area, stay seated at section 39

If you prefer to talk with Manna privately in your room, go to section 35

If you refuse to talk with Manna, say it in section 37

If you master the skill of sixth sense, feel what section 45 has for you...

33

You wake up at 8:00am, feeling well-rested, and very energized. You get up, give your body a good stretch, and look through your room window.

"Another beautiful sunny day has started…" you tell yourself.

You freshen up, get dressed, and leave your room to eat a good breakfast. This time, you are greeted by a waitress:

"Good morning. My name is Lalita. Please follow me."

You follow the waitress to yet another elegant table. As you sit down, she asks you:

"Would you be interested in trying a traditional Nepalese breakfast?"

"Certainly. What does it consist of?"

"I will serve you a traditional vegetable and potato soup, some fried bread, a fruit salad, and some *mahi* which is a buttermilk tea."

"Sounds lovely. Thank you."

As your waitress walks away, you are trying to imagine how you will manage to enter a time capsule…the ultimate fortress of time…

"Gutuk, I am counting on you," you tell yourself.

A few minutes later, your waitress is back with your food:

"Here it is," she says with a smile. "Enjoy our breakfast, and please do not hesitate to call me if you need anything else."

"Thank you very much."

Once again, your taste buds are not disappointed. The texture of the food is rich, the taste is delightful, and the combination of the fresh ingredients together, create a set of unique flavors in your mouth.

"What a treat!" you tell yourself.

At the end of your breakfast, you ask Lalita for your bill which she brings to you right away.

"I hope you enjoyed it," says your waitress.

"It was perfect."

You leave money on the table, and walk back to the hotel's front desk, thinking to yourself:

"I can't leave this hotel today. With everything that was brought to my attention, I feel that I will have to stay at least a few more days. I must listen to my gut."

You see an older man at the front desk, typing something on a computer.

"Pardon me Sir. I would like to stay at least three more nights in your hotel. I am in room twenty-four."

"Certainly. This will be arranged."

"Thank you Sir."

You pay the hotel employee for three more nights, and look at your watch.

"It's 9:00 o'clock."

You walk outside the main entrance, and see Ram waiting for you in his taxi.

"Good morning Ram."

"Good morning, young fakir."

"I am so sorry but there has been a last minute change of plans. I won't be able to leave with you today for Kang Guru Mountain."

"That's alright. These things happen."

"Do you have a phone number where I can reach you in the near future?"

"Of course. Here's my card."

"Thank you Ram. Here is one hundred rupees for your trouble."

"You don't have to do that."

"I want to. Once again thank you for everything, and I will be in touch."

"Thank you, young fakir."

You walk back into the hotel, and go straight to your room.

"Now, I must remain calm and concentrate. It's time for me to go back to the astral plane, and visit the akashic records."

You breathe deeply as you sit on the edge of the large bed. You then lie down, and relax your body before closing your eyes. Once again, you visualize your body becoming lighter and lighter, focusing on the infinite energy flowing all across your body. You start accelerating the movement of your body's molecules. Within seconds your molecules are vibrating so fast that your body becomes transparent before disappearing...

You feel your entire being fly higher and higher as you enter the now familiar tunnel of wonderful white light. At fabulous speed, your body is catapulted forward as you reach the splendid spirit world. A moment later, you are standing in the middle of that dazzling field you have learned to know as the akashic records.

"Good morning," says a familiar voice next to you.

"Good morning Gutuk." You recognize him immediately.

"How nice to see you again. Are you ready to lift the barrier of time?"

This is it!!! Get to section 38 now!

34

You hide behind the enormous rock against which you crashed years ago, and wait...but you don't have to wait too long. After a few minutes, you notice a group of about ten Tibetan monks, far away, walking in the snow, in your direction. Suddenly, they all stop walking, and look at your motionless body lying in the snow. They move in closer since they are unsure of what they see from such a distance. Suddenly, all the monks start to run towards your almost lifeless body. You immediately recognize all your Tibetan brothers as they get closer...

In no time, they surround your almost lifeless body, and look for your heartbeat. Without wasting any time, they quickly put together an improvised stretcher, and gently place you on it. As fast as they can, without jeopardizing your safety, they rush back to their lamasery. As you follow this beautiful scene from a distance, it brings tears to your eyes.

"I love you, my Tibetan family..."

Out of nowhere, you abruptly hear an unfamiliar sound. You turn around and notice a large cave, going inside the mountain, right behind you. Once again, you hear the same odd sound...somehow pleasant to the ear. Your natural sense of adventure sparks your curiosity even more!

If you want to take a peek inside the cave, walk to section 169...

If you prefer to travel back to see Gutuk, fly away to section 40...

35

"Let's go and talk in my room," you tell Manna. "This way we will have more privacy."

On your way to your room, you tell your waiter Bishal that you will be back very soon for your meal. You walk next to Manna until you reach your room. You then unlock the door, and let Manna pass in front of you. Inside, you each pull yourselves a comfortable chair, and sit down,

"I was sent to you by Gutuk and the High Priestess of Tibet, our common friends."

"How and when did you meet them?" you ask perplexed.

"That's a long story for another time I'm afraid. I live

outside Kathmandu with my seventeen-year-old granddaughter Shirisha. Two weeks ago, as you already know, the capital was shaken by a strong earthquake that took her parents' life. My granddaughter was at school when it happened. The roof collapsed on her and on some of her classmates, and fortunately she survived. Her right thigh was severely lacerated which resulted in a large wound that got quickly infected. I am doing what I can to take care of her but I do not have the proper medicine to help her heal, and the hospitals are running out of supplies.

"I am very sorry for your granddaughter."

"She keeps having a fever because her immune system is fighting the infection. Nevertheless, I am afraid that if I do not neutralize her infection soon, I might lose Shirisha."

"Tell me how I can help."

"You and I have both mastered the art of travelling to the akashic records, but I do not possess many of your other powers. One of the skills I learned from the High Priestess is teleporting my body anywhere, which you may also call molecular travel. I can also feel very deeply inside my soul, when someone is calling for me, and needs my help."

"I now see how you just appeared, out of nowhere, in front of me."

"In order to save Shirisha's life, I am asking you to travel to the akashic records, and enter one specific time capsule. Gutuk knows exactly which one. This time capsule will take you a thousand years back in time to Mount Fuji, in Japan. Back then, there used to be an unlimited amount of pink moss known as *shibazakura*, growing at the bottom of that mountain. A tiny amount of this pink moss, combined with *kurozu* - a common Japanese black vinegar - has the medicinal property to promptly cure all infections. I am asking you to get some of this pink moss for Shirisha, since I already have some *kurozu* from my last trip to Japan."

"It will be my pleasure to help you and your granddaughter," you kindly reply.

"I knew I could count on you, *Chosen One*. When Shirisha is back on her feet, it will be my turn to help you. When you successfully neutralize Sunita and her twin brother Raju, call for me wherever you are. I will immediately appear by your side. Then, I will show you how to take them with you to the akashic records in order for Gutuk to fix all the damage they have already done."

"Thank you in advance for helping me in my mission, Manna."

"No...I am the one who thanks you, *Chosen One*."

"My plan was to leave for Kang Guru Mountain tomorrow morning, but I will gladly put a hold on this plan to help you and your granddaughter. I see that her life is in jeopardy."

"Yes it is, but I feel we still have the time we need to save her. Now your priorities are to eat and rest. Otherwise, you will not be at your best."

"You are right Manna. Tomorrow morning, I will tell Ram, my taxi driver, that my plans have changed. From the privacy of my room, I will then travel to the akashic records. With Gutuk's help, I will enter the designated time capsule to propel myself back in time...a thousand years ago...to reach the base of Mount Fuji."

"You will succeed, *Chosen One*. I know you will. When you have the pink moss, please call for me...and I will appear."

"Thank you Manna."

She slowly disappears before your eyes. Feeling very excited by what you just heard, you get up and leave your room.

"*Time to eat!*" you think to yourself.

Just after sitting back at your table, your waiter Bishal shows up with your food:

"Here is your dal soup with your momo plate. The sauces are on this side plate."

"Thank you Bishal."

You are so absorbed by the discussion you just had, that you no longer feel hungry anymore, but you are quite curious to taste all these Nepalese delights in front of you.

"*Let's see what we have here...hhmmm...this soup is delicious! It's seasoned to perfection...and the momo plate is exquisite! How do they make these scrumptious sauces?*"

With a voracious appetite, you eat the delectable food brought to you, enjoying every bite of it. Bishal stops by your table, and asks:

"Is everything to your satisfaction?"

"Absolutely! It's simply luscious!"

A few minutes later, you are finished eating your meal. You ask Bishal to bring you your bill, and you pay it at once, leaving your waiter a very generous tip.

"Thank you so much!" says Bishal. "Have a very pleasant evening."

You go back to your room, thinking about the days ahead. You take a quick shower, and get ready for bed, feeling how tired you really are.

"*I have a big day tomorrow,*" you tell yourself.

In no time, you are in bed, and happy to finally get the rest you need.

Get ready for section 33!

36

About fifteen minutes later, you reach the famous Yak and Yeti Hotel. It's a very tall and wide luxurious building located in Nepal's beautiful capital: Kathmandu.

"Thank you for the ride," you tell Ram while giving him three hundred Nepalese rupees.

"Oh no! That's too much, young fakir. I can't accept that. This is more money than what I make in a month!"

"Please accept it. When I asked you to stop to help the young couple, you stopped. Another driver could have said 'no' and would have kept driving. You did the right thing, and I thank you for that."

"But YOU did the right thing. I just sat there and enjoyed seeing those men get knocked out cold!"

You change the subject, and tell Ram: "I need your help again."

"Anything for you."

"Could you drive me to Kang Guru Mountain?"

"Oh my dear young fakir! I would have loved to take you but I can't. It's not about the money, but about the road: there is no road that leads directly to Kang Guru Mountain. It's in a remote area of the country, about 145 km or 90 miles from Kathmandu. Why do you want to go there anyway?"

Ignoring his question, you ask Ram: "So...maybe there is a local airport near Kang Guru Mountain?"

"No there is not. Look...if it's so important for you, I suppose I could drive you half way. I have a friend, from a very wealthy family, who just opened a small hotel about 70 km or 45 miles from here. His name is Iok, and he has a helicopter. I'm sure he would be able to take you where you need to go."

"Thank you so much Ram! I gladly accept your offer, and would like to pay you double for driving me to see your friend."

"Double?"

"Yes, six hundred Nepalese rupees."

"You are too generous young fakir!"

"Could you please pick me up here in front of the main entrance tomorrow morning at 9:00am?"

"Absolutely," replies the driver.

"Thank you Ram. Drive safely, and I will see you tomorrow."

You shake hands with Ram, grab your backpack, and walk into the Yak and Yeti Hotel.

Enter the hotel at section 32

37

"How you managed to suddenly appear in front of me is a mystery, and I don't know you. Your unannounced presence makes me uncomfortable... and why are you calling me *The Chosen One*?"

"Tell me...how many times have you appeared unannounced, in this world or another one, to help someone in need? Many times...and I know this for a fact. Time is of essence, and we really need to talk. Shall we stay here or go to your room?"

Your instinct tells you that talking to this lady is imperative. You look deep inside her eyes, and finally say:

"Fine, let's talk..."

If you wish to stay in the dining area, stay seated at section 39

If you prefer to have a private talk with Manna in your room, go to section 35

38

"I am definitely ready," you tell Gutuk.

"*Chosen One*, you must understand that in the spirit world, your body will always be much more susceptible to react to any strong feelings you might have."

"What feelings?" you ask.

"Love, fear, passion, despair, sadness...to name a few...Such feelings are the key in breaking the barrier of time, for you to enter a time capsule. In addition, you must make your body's molecules move faster than ever, towards the scene you are witnessing."

"How do I do that?"

"It is different for each individual. In your case, I am asking you to watch...for the first time...the terrible accident that happened to you years ago...when your plane crashed above Tibet but you survived."

As Gutuk recalls this terrible incident, an atrocious feeling abruptly runs down your spine. He continues:

"You must relive this dreadful tragedy in order to wake up the appalling feelings sleeping inside you. Those feelings will propel you inside the time capsule. It is only then, after penetrating this time capsule, that you will be able to enter any time capsule of your choice. From the akashic virtual library or from another time capsule, you will only have to visualize what you want to see, and where you want to be. So if you want to go to Mount

Fuji, one thousand years back in time, simply visualize it."

Without further notice, a giant virtual blue screen unexpectedly appears in front of you, and your heart starts pounding inside your chest. Suddenly, the screen turns black, and you see the plane which you were on, flying through that dark cold night. The aircraft is relentlessly shaken by the strong Himalayan winds which reminds you of the fear you felt at that moment. Out of nowhere, you see one of its engines burst into flames, as the plane starts tipping forward before free-falling above Tibet. A few seconds later, you witness the terrible explosion which split the aircraft right open, pulverizing everything inside, killing the passengers and crew members, and ejecting you into the obscure and freezing night...

As you watch in horror these wretched scenes, you are suddenly seized by uncontrollable convulsions. Reliving the biggest tragedy of your life awakens extreme feelings of fear, panic, anger, sadness...Your body' molecules start to vibrate at a mind-blowing speed! All of a sudden, you scream like never before as you feel your pulsating body being sucked into that time capsule.

A few seconds later, you open your eyes...and realize you are lying face down in the thick snow. You get up, and a short distance away, you see yourself...but it is your other self, from many years ago, lying in the snow with a fractured bloody skull.

"I'm in..." you tell yourself, *"I have entered this time capsule...my time capsule! I did it!"*

**If you wish to stay and watch how you were
rescued by your Tibetan family, stay at section 34**

If you prefer to go back to see Gutuk, travel to section 40

39

Manna sees that you are staying seated, so she continues:

"I was sent to you by Gutuk and the High Priestess of Tibet, our mutual friends."

"How and when did you meet them?" you ask perplexed.

"That's a long story for another time I'm afraid. I live outside Kathmandu with my seventeen-year-old granddaughter Shirisha. Two weeks ago, as you know, the capital was shaken by a strong earthquake that took her parents' life. My granddaughter was at school when it happened. The roof collapsed on her, and onto some of her classmates. Unfortunately, they perished and only she survived. She suffered a large wound on her right thigh which quickly got infected. I am currently doing what I can to take care of her but I do not have the proper medicine, and the hospitals are running out of supplies."

"I am very sorry for your granddaughter."

"She keeps getting a fever because her immune system is fighting the infection. Nevertheless, I am afraid that if I do not neutralize her infection soon, Shirisha might die."

"Please tell me how I can help."

"You and I have both mastered the art of travelling to the akashic records, but I do not possess your powers. One of the skills that I have learned from the High Priestess, which I'm sure you are familiar with, is teleporting my body, also known as molecular travel. The second skill I have is to be able to sense deeply inside my soul when someone is calling for me, and needs my immediate help."

"Wow! I now see and understand how you suddenly appeared in front of me."

"Now, in order to save Shirisha's life, I am seeking your help. I need you to travel to the akashic records, and enter one specific time capsule. Gutuk knows exactly which one. This time capsule will take you one thousand years back in time to Mount Fuji, in Japan. Back then, there used to be an unlimited amount of pink moss, known as *shibazakura*, growing at the base of that mountain. A tiny amount of this pink moss, combined with a common Japanese black vinegar called *kurozu*, have the medicinal property to promptly cure all infections. All I am asking is for you to bring back some of this pink moss, since I already have some *kurozu* from my last trip to Japan."

"It would be my pleasure to help you and your granddaughter," you kindly reply.

"I knew I could count on you, *Chosen One*. When Shirisha is back on her feet, it will be my turn to help you. When you successfully neutralize Sunita and her twin brother Raju, please call for me. I will immediately appear by your side. Then, I will help you take them to the akashic records, in order for Gutuk to fix all the damage they have already caused."

"Thank you in advance for helping me in my mission, Manna."

"No...I am the one who thanks you, *Chosen One*."

"My plan was to leave for Kang Guru Mountain tomorrow morning, but I will gladly put a hold on this plan to help you and your granddaughter. Her life is in jeopardy as we speak."

"Yes it is, but I feel we still have the time we need to save her. Now your priorities are to eat and rest. Otherwise, you will not be at your best."

"You are right Manna. Tomorrow morning, I will tell Ram, my taxi driver, that my plans have changed, and I will cancel my trip with him. Instead, in the privacy of my room, I will then travel to the akashic records. With Gutuk's help, I will enter the designated time capsule to propel myself back in time...a thousand years ago...to reach the bottom of Mount Fuji."

"You will succeed, *Chosen One*. I know you will! Once you have the pink moss and you are back in your hotel room, please call for me...I will appear."

"Thank you Manna."

She slowly disappears before your eyes. A moment later, your waiter Bishal shows up with your food:

"Here is your dal soup with your momo plate. The sauces are on this side plate."

"Thank you Bishal."

You are so absorbed by the discussion you just had that you don't really feel hungry anymore. However, you are quite curious to taste all these Nepalese delights in front of you.

"Let's see what we have here...hhmmm...this soup is delicious! It's seasoned to perfection...and the momo plate is exquisite! How do they make these scrumptious sauces?"

With a voracious appetite, you eat the delectable food brought to you, enjoying every bite of it. Bishal stops by your table, and asks:

"Is everything to your satisfaction?"

"Absolutely! It's simply delicious!"

A few minutes later, you are done eating your meal. You ask Bishal to bring you your bill, and you pay it at once, leaving your waiter a very generous tip.

"Thank you so much!" says Bishal. "Have a very pleasant evening."

You go back to your room, thinking about the days ahead. You take a quick shower, and get ready for bed, feeling how tired you really are.

"*I have a big day tomorrow*," you tell yourself.

In no time, you are in bed, happy to finally get the rest you need.

Get ready for section 33!

40

You close your eyes, and visualize that you are once again back in the akashic records' virtual library. A few seconds later, you are standing inside a limitless field where the most stunning bright light fills the air. You notice Gutuk floating next to you, and smiling at you.

"Congratulations, *Chosen One*. You did it! I knew you would be successful."

"Thank you Gutuk. I found it to be a very intense experience. I'm glad it's behind me."

"Are you ready for your next trip?"

"Absolutely. I must go back in time one thousand years..."

"How do you feel about that?"

"I feel very excited. I have never been to Japan in my life. But...how will I communicate with people? I don't speak Japanese... and I don't have any Japanese clothes, especially from that era. What am I to do?"

"I forgot to mention one detail: every time you travel back

in time, your body adapts itself entirely to the time capsule. In other words, as soon as you step inside a time capsule, you automatically become appropriately attired for the occasion, and you immediately master the language being used."

"Amazing!" you simply say.

"Let me remind you that if need be, you may use your magical skills."

"I will remember that Gutuk. Wish me luck!"

"You don't need luck, *Chosen One*."

You close your eyes, relax your being, and start visualizing yourself standing at the bottom of Mount Fuji, one thousand years ago...

A few seconds later, you open your eyes, and you are standing at the bottom of a spectacular mountain. As you look up, the view is so impressive...as if the mountain's peak was piercing the sky.

"I am in Japan!"

Enjoy the view until section 46!

41

"Good day to you, powerful warriors," you tell the group of samurai as you slightly bow to them, and invite the twins to do the same.

"I'm not bowing to these clowns dressed in Halloween costumes," says Raju.

"You must show them respect, Raju," whispers Sunita.

"They're not showing us any respect by yelling at us!" answers the teenager.

"BOW TO US AT ONCE!" yells one of the samurai looking at Raju.

"Why should I do that?" responds the arrogant teenager.

An older samurai quickly walks up to Raju, and tries to slap him across the face, but the young martial art expert sweeps his hand, and throws the samurai to the ground. Furious, the samurai swiftly gets up, yanks out his sword, and lifts it above his own head in an attempt to slay the young man. At the last possible second, you stop the warrior by grabbing one of his arms as you say to him:

"No! Honorable samurai, please have mercy on him. This young man may be foolish and arrogant, but he means no harm. He does not yet control the words that fly out of his mouth. I apologize on his behalf."

The older warrior looks at you, and puts his sword back in its sheath. He then screams:

"So teach him some manners! Otherwise he will get himself killed!"

"Yes, honorable samurai," you quickly answer.

From the back of the group, a middle-aged samurai slowly walks up to you, his piercing eyes analyzing your facial features. Calmly, he asks you:

"Who are you, and why are you here?"

"Please call me *Cho*, honorable samurai. We are simple travelers, and we come from a faraway land. We heard of this pink moss called *shibazakura* which can be found at the bottom if this mountain. We were told it can heal any infection. To help the people we care about, we traveled to your land to get some of this pink moss."

The powerful samurai looks at you for a moment in utter silence. He then speaks:

"I admire your honesty, courage, and altruism. These are rare qualities to find in people. You jumped in front of a sword to save your friend from an imminent death. Not many samurai would have done that."

"Thank you for your kind words, honorable samurai."

"My name is Kenji."

"It is an honor to meet you, Kenji-san," you say as you bow again to the samurai.

"Kenji what?" asks Raju.

"Stop talking!" says Sunita to her brother. "You are going to get us all killed!"

Kenji slowly walks up to Raju, and says:

"I do not like you. You are rude, and arrogant. We must teach you a lesson." Kenji slowly walks away, staring at the ground, then comes back to face Raju, and says:

"Instead of killing you on the spot for your arrogance, I will give you a chance to live: you have to guess who is the highest ranking samurai among us. Guess correctly and you will live. If you give me the wrong answer, my friend Sawato, master of the bow, will send you straight to hell with an arrow to your chest..."

"WHAT?" says Raju.

"Please have mercy on him," begs Sunita.

"Honorable Kenji-san," you say, "thank you for giving him a chance to live. But with your permission, I would like to accept this challenge. This young man is not ready for it, and will end up dead. Please allow me, on his behalf, to try to fix his mistake."

Very surprised to hear such a request, Kenji looks at you for a moment without saying a word. He then says:

"Once again, you are willing to risk your life for your friend. You are impressing me more and more, Cho-san. Your bravery is exemplary. I grant you your request, but it will be a shame to watch you die. Before you tell me what I need to hear, I must tell you something that might confuse you even more: I am not the highest ranking samurai here."

All the other eleven samurai abruptly walk away from you, turn around, and line up one next to the other, facing you. Among them, you see Sawato, the *yumi* or bow master, ready to fire a *ya* at you...in other words an arrow! Kenji then says:

"Now tell me: who is the highest ranking samurai amongst my friends?"

If you choose:

the first samurai to your left, good luck at section 50

to use your sixth sense because you mastered this skill, run to section 105

the eight samurai, run to section 70

the tenth samurai, prepare yourself for section 55

the fifth samurai, walk to section 60

the seventh samurai, turn to section 95

the third samurai, sneak up to section 65

the eleventh samurai, choose section 75

the sixth samurai, run to section 100

the second samurai, discover section 80

to talk about the significance of friendship, section 110 is for you

the fourth samurai, get ready for section 85

the ninth samurai, simply go to section 90

42

You breathe very deeply, feeling the energy around you and in the air. It's the same creative energy which exists in all life forms. You feel this warm energy penetrating every molecule of your body, filling it up completely. You then direct all this accumulated energy around your forearm while executing a large circular movement with your arm. Instantaneously, you are holding the impenetrable shield of heaven!

A massive fight explodes around you as you start running towards a ninja throwing *shurikens* at you, which are sharp metal stars. You easily block the projectiles with your heavenly shield. Just before reaching him, you jump high into the air before smashing your shield into the ninja's abdomen. Another hit from you knocks him out completely. You then run towards Kenji, who is suddenly fighting two ninjas at the same time! You jump off the ground, literally flying through the air, and land a fantastic flying side kick across the jaw of one of the ninjas!

You land on the ground, ready to continue the fight. You look around but the battle is already over. All the samurai are still alive, and are putting back their swords inside their sheaths, satisfied with the outcome.

Continue your journey at section 58

43

You instantly activate the windy magical flow inside you, as you start spinning extremely fast in the spot where you are standing. You open your arms to expand the magnitude of what you are becoming... You are now spinning so fast that you become invisible, creating all around your body an extremely powerful whirlwind...and transforming your-self into an immense tornado!

You slide very quickly towards all the ninjas who cannot understand what is suddenly happening. One after the other, you touch them with your powerful whirlwind, and catapult them into the air in all possible directions.

A few minutes later, you stop spinning, and are back to your normal self. All the ninjas are on the ground, completely knocked out, and the twelve samurai are looking at you in dismay.

It's time to go to section 59

44

Breathing deeply, you feel a huge flow of magic passing through your entire body, as your hands become very hot and steamy. Without more ado, you send a giant iron bolt towards two ninjas, making the bolt roll on the ground at great speed. Your opponents barely have time to jump out of the way, wondering where these big metal spheres came from. You quickly send two more rolling bolts towards other ninjas, and manage to squash a few

toes! But your opponents are tough, and keep running forward. In no time, a few ninjas reach the samurai, while three of them are coming straight at you.

"Let's change my tactic," you tell yourself.

You start shooting smaller iron bolts at the ninjas' legs, hitting their shins and thighs with great force. The ninjas drop to the ground like flies, holding their bruised legs, and feeling immense pain. The samurai fight with amazing vigor and determination, not leaving a single chance of victory to their opponents. A moment later, the fight is over, but the samurai are still amazed by what they have seen you accomplish!

Walk to section 61

45

Your remarkable sixth sense warns you that if you refuse to talk this older lady, you will be making a very big mistake!!!

If you wish to stay in the dining area, stay seated at section 39

If you prefer to go speak with Manna in your room, go to section 35

46

Admiring the breathtaking scenery, you look around. The air is brisk and fresh, the trees are big, healthy, and strong. Many colourful birds fly through the air, chasing each other as they twirl in the clear blue sky.

"What a stunning place," you tell yourself.

Instinct. You turn around and, a few feet away, notice two older teenagers - a girl and a guy - looking at you. Like you, they are wearing Japanese kimonos, but look Nepalese. You overhear their conversation:

"Sunita," says the young man, "did you see what I saw?"

The young lady keeps staring at you

with great interest, and says:

"Yes Raju. This person just 'magically' appeared in front of us!"

"Sunita? Raju? No way! I'm in the presence of the Nepalese twins whom I have to stop! What a coincidence! I obviously can't reveal who I really am, but I have to make them trust me so they drop down their guard. They saw me appear in front of them, so I can't hide my ability to travel back in time. Nevertheless, I need to bluff a little bit..."

You decide to take a few steps towards the twins, and say in English:

"All right you two! Let me get right to the point: you and I are from the same era. You can call me *Cho*...All of us have travelled back in time over one thousand years in order to be here. I know you are twins, and you live in Nepal, probably in Kathmandu. You hired an army of workers to build you a palace at the bottom of Kang Guru Mountain. There! Did I leave anything out?"

"How do you know all of this about us?" asks Sunita very perplexed.

"People talk," you simply answer. "The word gets around fast. In our era, with all the social media and gadgets, it doesn't take much for information to go viral..."

"How did you get here?" continues Sunita.

"The same way you did," you simply answer.

"You mean you entered a time capsule by accident?" asks Raju.

"You just took the words out of my mouth," you tell the tall teenage boy.

"Who taught you how to travel to the Akashic records in the first place? Your parents?" continues Sunita.

"Once again, you just took the words out of my mouth!"

"Why are you here?" says Raju.

"Judging by the pink moss that you are holding, something tells me that I am here for the same reason as you are."

"Our mother suffers from a severe chronic throat infection," says Sunita. "This *shibazakura* will heal her."

"I too want to help someone heal. That's why I am here."

"HEY YOU THREE!" says a menacing voice. You all turn around...and see a dozen samurai glaring at you, ready to take out their swords.

"This is not good..." you tell the twins.

Get ready for section 41!

47

"I must stop them COLD!" you tell yourself, as you activate a fantastic flow of magic inside your body.

"SWORDS OUT!" yells Kenji.

But before the ninjas can reach you and the samurai, you throw giant ice bolts at the first four ninjas. They all abruptly fall to the ground, their entire bodies suddenly trapped in a thick ice  block! The other ninjas unexpectedly stop running, their gaze now fixed on you. Without any warning, you send a fast flurry of large ice bolts at three more ninjas, freezing them on the spot, from their shoulders down. The remaining ninjas prefer running away, understanding that fighting against you is futile. Kenji looks at you in awe, as he walks up to a frozen ninja, and says:

"When this ice melts, go back to your clan, and tell everyone about what just happened. Spread the word: the samurai will exterminate all ninjas if you keep attacking us."

Kenji then slowly turns to you with an approving smile on his face...

Section 66 is next!

48

A tall muscular ninja throws a sharp metal star at you but you jump high into the air to avoid being hit...and start flying! At great speed, you glide through the air over the ninjas' heads, threatening to crash into them. Suddenly, you fly towards a stocky ninja before grabbing him by the arms, and lifting him off the ground. Seized with panic, he wiggles through the air but you hold him very tightly. You then fly low, straight in front of you, and decide to drop the wiggly ninja onto one of his ninja buddies! Scared for their lives, all ninjas start to run back towards the mountain, obviously seeing they don't stand a chance against such an opponent like you.

"I see they got the message," you tell yourself. All the samurai stare at you in disbelief.

It's time for section 68

49

As the ninjas run towards you and the twelve samurai, you activate your unique telekinetic ability. Without delay, you stretch your arms out in front of you, and slowly lift them up. At the same time, all the ninjas are lifted high above the ground, and now look like panicked wiggling puppets. You move them through the air, far away from you, before dropping them all at the top of Mount Fuji!

"I don't believe they will be coming back today," you tell Kenji. The samurai and the other warriors simply gawk at you in disbelief.

Walk to section 72

50

You carefully look at all eleven samurai facing you, wondering which one to pick. After a long while, you tell Kenji:

"The highest ranking samurai is the first one to my left."

With a very disappointed look, Kenji tells you:

"You guessed wrong, Cho-san."

An arrow is fired your way, but you catch it in mid-air just before it is about to pierce your chest. You throw it to the ground as you look at Kenji, and say:

"I don't believe I deserve to die because of a wrong answer."

Suddenly, a very long poisoned arrow hits you from the back.

"NINJAS!" yells a samurai. "DEFEND YOUR LIVES!"

Those are the last words you will ever hear...

THE END

51

"I must stop this attack before it becomes a bloody confrontation," you think to yourself. *"All our lives are in great danger!"*

Raising up both of your arms so that the ninjas see you, you send them an exceptionally loud telepathic message which resonates in their heads like the loudest bells:

"STOP RIGHT NOW!" you order them. "I COMMAND YOU TO GO BACK TO WHERE YOU CAME FROM IN ORDER TO STAY ALIVE!"

All ninjas instantly stop running, and grab their heads with two hands, screaming in pain. Not understanding what is happening to them but feeling as if their heads are about to explode, they listen to your order. They turn around, and run for their lives in the direction they came from.

"This is better, don't you think Kenji-san?" you ask the samurai. He looks at you, feeling utterly confused by what just happened.

Go to section 71

52

You stare at the ninjas running towards you, as you open an incredible flow of magic inside your being. You see your opponents holding swords and other weapons. Unexpectedly, powerful fire jets come out of your hands, as you shoot them precisely at your opponents' weapons. The fire blaze crashes into the steel, slightly burning the ninjas' hands. They abruptly stop running, gawking at you in disbelief.

"RUN AWAY IF YOU WANT TO LIVE!" you yell at the warriors dressed in black. Immediately, you shoot another burst of fire jets at them, sending blazes at their feet. Fearing for their lives, and thinking you are some kind of sorcerer, that appeared from the underworld, the ninjas start running back to where they came from!

"No damage done," you tell yourself. You then notice that all twelve samurai are slowly walking towards you, an incredulous expression painted on their faces...

Time for section 67!

53

Swiftly, your body starts to become more and more transparent before becoming invisible. Immediately, you start running towards the ninjas, leaving the speechless samurai behind you.

"How is this possible?" wonders Kenji. "Cho simply disappeared before my eyes...like magic!"

An impressive battle explodes all around you between the samurai and the ninjas. Both groups display an extraordinary array of techniques and endurance, as they fight vigorously. You see Kenji fighting two ninjas at once when he is suddenly thrown to the ground. One of his two opponents pulls out a throwing knife but before he can use it, the edge of your palm strikes him like a blade behind the neck, knocking him out cold. Without more ado, you throw a powerful reverse roundhouse kick to the other ninja's jaw, sending him unconscious to the ground. You abruptly reappear in front of Kenji. He looks at you, obviously very confused.

"I don't understand," he says in a very low voice. "How did you..."

"CROUCH!" you yell at him.

The samurai throws himself to the ground as you jump over him to deliver a fantastic flying kick to a ninja behind him. He crumbles to the ground in a silent moan, dropping his deadly sword. A moment later, the fight is over. You see all the samurai put their swords back into their sheaths.

It's time for section 69...

54

"Are you ready for this?" asks you Kenji.

"I am."

Before the ninjas are able to reach any of the samurai, you start blasting powerful red laser beams from your eyes! You aim right at the ninjas' legs to avoid killing them, and to scare them away. Your plan works like a charm! Seized by panic, all ninjas start to run away, thinking you are some kind of dangerous mythical creature that appeared from the underworld.

"That was a really short confrontation," you tell yourself. Only then, you notice that all samurai are staring at you with a mix of admiration and fear in their eyes.

Continue your journey to section 62

55

For a long time you stare at all eleven samurai facing you, doing your best to guess correctly. You then suddenly say:

"I know: the highest ranking samurai is the tenth one."

"I am sorry, Cho-san," replies Kenji.

An arrow is fired towards your chest, but you catch it in mid-air. You break it in half, and throw it to the ground:

"Kenji-san, I deserve to live, not die!"

Suddenly, a poisoned meter-long arrow hits you between the shoulder blades. You fall face first to the ground.

"NINJAS ARE ATTACKING US!" yells Sawato. "FIGHT!"

In your case...you are already dead.

THE END

56

You start running towards two ninjas that are coming your way. They throw sharp metal stars at you, but you duck and roll to the ground with great agility, not to be hit. You are about to reach the two warriors of the night when you are tackled from the back by a third ninja! To his great surprise, you easily throw the man over your shoulder, and strike him with two fingers at the base of his neck, paralyzing your opponent instantaneously! You immediately turn around and duck, avoiding a vicious roundhouse kick about to pulverize your jaw. You launch towards the

 second ninja, and strike him behind the knee with your thumb. The ninja crumbles to the ground, screaming in pain, his leg now paralyzed from the knee down. You take him out of his misery by hitting a specific spot on his chest, abruptly knocking him out cold. The last ninja stares at you with anger as he slowly pulls out his sword.

"You pull out a sword to fight an unarmed person?" says a familiar voice behind you. You turn around, and see Kenji next to four other samurai. "Fight me instead!"

The ninja looks at Kenji, at you, and at the other samurai coming his way. Out of his sleeve, he quickly takes out a small metal sphere, and throws it in front of him. When the sphere hits the ground, it creates a small explosion followed by a thick cloud of smoke. A few seconds later, the smoke has disappeared...and so has the ninja!

Continue your journey at section 63

57

Before you know it, a very imposing ninja jumps right at you, holding a sword above his head. You deflect one of his arms holding the sword before grabbing it, and making the ninja spin around you. In a spectacular throw, you smash your opponent to the ground with great force, knocking him out. Keeping his sword in your hand, you are suddenly faced with another ninja who throws a long metal chain at your sword. You hit the chain with your weapon, and jump towards the ninja, landing a fantastic spinning back kick across his jaw. He has nowhere to go but down.

Ready to continue, you look around but the battle is already over. With all the ninjas down on the ground, the twelve samurai are calmly putting back their swords inside their sheaths, happy to be alive.

Calmly continue your journey at section 64

58

Slowly, Kenji walks up to you and says:

"Who are you...really?"

"I am a person, just like you," you simply answer.

"No you are not, Cho-san. I cannot make a shield magically appear on my forearm, but you can. Are you some kind of super celestial being with magical powers?"

"I can assure you I am no super celestial being. I am human like you and your friends. I do have special skills, and those were taught to me a long time ago...far away from here..."

"I would love to learn more about you, Cho-san. Today, you saved my life when you caught that arrow about to pierce my throat. I do not know how you did it but you did. Let me thank you...the samurai way..."

Listen to Kenji at section 76

59

Sawato, master of the bow, looks at you from a distance, and asks nervously:

"How did you do that? How did you transform yourself into a tornado?"

"I have learned special skills a long time ago...far away from here."

"I don't believe you, Cho-san. You must be some kind of celestial super being."

"I can assure you that I am not. I am a human, just like you and the other samurai."

"So, how can you catch flying arrows?" asks another warrior.

"As I told you, I have acquired special skills during my life. There is nothing more to it."

Kenji puts his hand on your shoulder, and says:

"I do not know what to think about what I have witnessed today, Cho-san. You did save my life when you caught that arrow about to pierce my throat. How you did it is a mystery to me. Allow me to thank you...the samurai way..."

Go to section 76

60

You focus on all the samurai standing before you, studying their facial expressions. You finally say:

"The highest ranking samurai is the fifth one."

Kenji looks down at the ground as he tells you:

"Goodbye, Cho-san."

An arrow is fired your way, but you intercept it in mid-air before it pierces your flesh. You jam it into the ground, and say:

"You all want to live...and so do I."

Suddenly, a very long poisoned arrow hits you from the back, and lodges itself deep into your spine.

"NINJAS!" yells Kenji. "TAKE OUT YOUR SWORDS!"

You can't join the fight because for you, it is...

THE END

61

"Before today, I have never seen iron bolts magically appear between a person's hands," says Kenji. "You must be some kind of super being sent by our ancestors."

"No I am not, Kenji-san. I am just a person like you," you simply answer.

"No you are not, Cho-san. I cannot make iron bolts magically appear between my hands, but you can."

"I can assure you I am no super being sent by your ancestors. I am human like you and the other samurai. I do have special skills, and those were taught to me a long time ago...far away from here..."

"I want to believe you, Cho-san, but I guess it does not matter at this point. Today, you saved my life when you caught that arrow about to pierce my throat. I don't know how you did it but you did. Let me thank you...the samurai way..."

Listen to Kenji at section 76

62

Kenji slowly walks up to you and says:

"Can you explain what just happened, Cho-san?"

"Yes, Kenji-san. During my life, I have acquired special skills and powers that I sometimes use for the good of mankind. I am really just a human being like you," you answer.

"Cho-san, we all saw red burning lights coming out of your eyes, and you can catch flying arrows. I certainly cannot do all these things. You must be some kind of super celestial being with magical powers."

"No Kenji-san. I assure you I am no super celestial being. I am a person, just like you and your friends. I do have special skills, and those were taught to me a long time ago...far away from here..."

"Why didn't you kill all ten ninjas with your red light?" asks Sawato, the bow master.

"I want to preserve life," you simply answer. "I refuse to kill people. I will neutralize my opponents if need be, but I will not take their lives away."

"That's very noble, Cho-san. When I saw you earlier, I knew your heart was pure. Now, allow me to thank you for saving my life..."

It is time for section 76

63

Kenji slowly walks up to you and says:

"Cho-san...I want to know who you really are."

"I am a human being, like you," you answer.

"I do not believe that. Your combat skills are outstanding, and you can catch flying arrows - I certainly cannot. Are you some sort of super warrior with magical powers?"

"No Kenji-san. I am a person, just like you and your samurai friends. I do have special skills, but those were taught to me a long time ago...far away from here..."

"Today, you saved my life Cho-san, and I will never forget that. Allow me to properly thank you...like a real samurai does..."

Prepare yourself for section 76

64

Kenji slowly walks up to you and says:

"Who are you, Cho-san?"

"I am a human being, like you," you answer.

"I doubt that. Your hand-to-hand combat skills are exceptional, and YOU can catch flying arrows - I certainly cannot. Are you some sort of super celestial being with magical powers?"

"No Kenji-san. I assure you I am no super celestial being. I am a person just like you and the other samurai. I do have some special skills, and those were taught to me a long time ago...far away from here..."

"I would love to hear your story, Cho-san. Today, you saved my life, and you helped us all. Let me thank you...the samurai way..."

Walk to section 76

65

You observe very carefully all the samurai in front of you, trying to sense which one to pick. With a smile on your face, you tell Kenji:

"The highest ranking warrior here is the third samurai."

Disappointed, Kenji tells you:

"There is no place here for mistakes, Cho-san."

A deadly arrow is fired your way, but you catch it before it reaches you, to your audience's disbelief! You walk up to Kenji, and say:

"I believe I paid a high enough price for your honor."

Unexpectedly, you stop breathing, and fall into Kenji's arms after a very long poisoned arrow hits you in the back.

"NINJAS!" yells a samurai. "WE ARE UNDER ATTACK!"

You tried your best...

THE END

66

"Please explain yourself, Cho-san," says Kenji with a calm but nervous voice.

"Yes, Kenji-san. During my life, I have acquired special skills and powers. When I need to do so, I use my special abilities but only for the good of mankind. I am really just an ordinary person like you."

"Cho-san, we all saw you throwing ice bolts with your hands, and catching an arrow ripping through the air. I certainly cannot do all these things. You must be some sort of super celestial being with magical powers."

"I assure you that I am no such being, Kenji-san. I am a person like you and your samurai friends. I do have special skills, and those were taught to me a long time ago...far away from here..."

"I do not know what to think of what you are telling me, but I know that I will be eternally grateful to you for saving my life. Allow me to thank you personally..."

Walk with Kenji to section 76

67

Sawato, master of the bow, yells out in your direction:

"You had fire coming out of your hands! How did you do that? Are you a wizard??!"

"No, Sawato-san," you answer in a calm voice. "I have simply acquired special skills and powers during my life. It happened far away from here, and a long time ago...."

"I don't believe you, Cho-san. You must then be a *Kami* - a mystical being with super powers - sent to us from our ancestors."

"I assure you, I am not. I am human, just like you and the other samurai."

"So how can you catch deadly arrows ripping through the air?" asks another warrior.

"As I told you, I have acquired special skills."

Kenji looks at his samurai friends and says:

"Cho-san is right. A wizard could have killed us by now, but it is not the case. We are all well, and alive." The samurai then glances at you, and says: "The fact is that you did save my life today. For that, I owe you. Allow me to thank you personally..."

Prepare for section 76

68

A short and agile samurai apprehensively walks up to you, gets down on one knee before you, and says:

"Master, you were sent to us by our ancestors to help us. You are a super celestial being, and I thank you from the bottom of my heart for helping us the way you did."

As the man says these words, all the other samurai abruptly kneel before you, and bow their heads forward.

"Please, you don't need to bow," you modestly state. "I am no such being. Why would you think so?"

"You can fly like a bird," replies another samurai. "Only a celestial super being could do so."

"I can assure you I am no such being. During my life, I have acquired special skills, and powers through intense training. That is all."

"So how come you catch flying arrows?" asks another warrior.

"As I told you, I have special training."

Kenji stares at you with incredible admiration in his eyes, and says:

"Bird or not, you did save my life when you caught that arrow about to pierce my throat. How you did, and how you learned to fly is a mystery to me. Nevertheless, allow me to thank you...the samurai way..."

Go to section 76

69

Kenji's gaze dives deep into yours as he says:

"Cho-san, you magically disappeared before my eyes, and knocked out two ninjas before reappearing, and neutralizing a third one. Becoming invisible, as you did, is incomprehensible to me. Would you care to explain yourself?"

"During my life, Kenji-san, I have acquired special powers and skills to help humanity. What you saw today is part of what I have learned."

"So you are not some kind of sorcerer or super being?"

"No, I am not. I am simply human, just like you."

"Cho-san," goes on Sawato, "we all saw you disappear. I certainly can't do it. Maybe you are a master of black magic!"

"I assure you that I am not, Sawato-san. I am a person...like you and your samurai friends. I fought with you against the ninjas, didn't I?"

"I do not know what to think of what you are telling us, but I know that I will always be grateful for you saving my life," says Kenji. "Allow me to thank you personally..."

Walk with Kenji to section 76

70

You take your time to make your decision. You look very carefully at all the samurai, studying their armor, weapons, and behaviour. You finally tell Kenji:

"The highest ranking warrior here is the eighth samurai."

"Are you sure?" enquires Kenji.

A deadly arrow is fired your way, but you catch it in mid-air to your audience's dismay. You run up to Kenji, and say:

"I want to live just as much as you do. I have paid my dues."

Without warning, you suddenly feel a sharp pain between your shoulder blades. You stop breathing, and fall at Kenji's feet: a long poisoned arrow just pierced you!

"NINJAS!" yells Kenji. "EVERYONE GRAB YOUR SWORDS!"

Unfortunately for you, your mission will never be completed because it is...

THE END

71

Measuring his steps, Kenji walks up to you and says in an incredulous voice:

"Did you have anything to do with this...with the ninjas running away?"

"Yes. I am able to send people messages with my mind. As you saw, I just sent a very effective command to the ninjas to make them run back to where they came from."

"Who are you Cho-san?"

"I am a person, just like you," you simply answer.

"No you are not. I cannot send people messages with my mind, but you can. Are you some kind of super celestial being with magical powers?"

"I assure you that I am not. I am human, like you and your samurai friends. I do have special skills, and those were taught to me a long time ago...far away from here..."

"Well Cho-san, today, you saved my life when you caught that arrow about to pierce my throat. I see it is another skill you have, and I am guessing you have many more. Now let me thank you personally..."

Go to section 76

72

"Cho-san," asks you Kenji, "did you just magically move all the ninjas, through the air, before dumping them on top of Mount Fuji?"

"Yes I did," you kindly answer.

"I am flabbergasted by your accomplishment. Are you a celestial creature sent to us by our ancestors?"

"No, Kenji-san. In my life, I have acquired special powers and skills to help people. What you saw today is part of what I have learned."

"I find that hard to believe. You must be an angel or a magical sorcerer."

"No, I am not. I am simply a human, just like you."

"Let us discuss this later. The bottom line is that you saved my life, and now I must return the favour. Let me thank you as it should be done."

Walk with Kenji to section 76

73

Out of nowhere, you see Sunita and Raju walking in your direction. Kenji and his samurai turn around to face the newcomers.

"Sorry we missed the fun," says Raju with an insolent voice. "Wow! Nice sword!" he yaps at you. "Can I have it?"

"Quiet Raju!" says his sister. She bows to the samurai, and forces her brother to do the same.

"We are sorry we left but we quickly had to bring the pink moss for our mother. As we speak, a special ointment is being prepared for her by our father, and she will finally be able to heal from her throat infection."

"How did you manage to leave and come back so quickly?" asks Kenji perplexed.

"We ran...really fast! Ha! Ha! Ha!" blurs out Raju.

Kenji fixes the young man with a cold gaze. He takes a few seconds to think before he finally says:

"I really do not like you, young man."

"My name is Raju by the way," replies the teen.

"I have never met such an arrogant, rude, and impolite young man in my life," continues Kenji.

"That's because you haven't lived long enough," Raju defends himself.

Sawato immediately grabs his bow and an arrow, but Kenji motions his friend to stop by simply raising his hand. He then addresses Raju:

"You definitively need to learn a lesson young man. Are you a good fighter?"

"In hand-to-hand combat, I'm the best...and my name is Raju!"

Kenji then looks at you and continues:

"Cho-san, as a sign of my gratitude to you, I would be honored to invite you and your friends to my Daimyo's palace. His name is Oda Nobunaga. In three days, in honor of our Shogun..."

"What is Daimyo and who is Shogun?" insolently interrupts the detestable young man.

Kenji looks at him in disbelief, but very serenely answers:

"The Daimyo is one of the Shogun's vassals who hired us, the samurai, to care for his land,

and defend it in the Shogun's name. The Shogun is our emperor...As I was saying before being rudely interrupted, my Daimyo is organizing our annual martial arts tournament. The best samurai in the entire province will get to test their great fighting skills against one another."

Kenji's eyes then dive into yours as he continues:

"Since you saved my life in combat, you therefore have the right to participate in this competition...and your friends, by affiliation to you, have the same right. Now, do you accept my invitation?"

"Yes, Kenji-san. I would be honored to participate in such a prestigious tournament."

"The honor is mine, Cho-san," replies Kenji.

"So...how do I win a fight, Kenji?" enquires Raju.

"It's Kenji-san!" whispers Sunita as she nudges him. "It's a mark of respect."

"By submission - meaning when your opponent gives up - or by knock out," answers Kenji as he looks at the young lady.

"I'm so going to win this!" says Raju.

"We shall see..." replies Kenji.

"Kenji-san, forgive me, but I must now pick some *shibazakura* at the base of Mount Fuji, and bring it to a young lady who is suffering. Her life actually depends on this rare pink moss. With your permission, I will now be on my way, and do what I have to. But, I promise to be back in three days, in time for the tournament."

"Very well," answers Kenji. "You will find our Daimyo's palace on the other side of Mount Fuji. We will see you in three days. Until then Cho-san..."

"Yes you will, Kenji-san."

"We'll be there too!" yells Raju. "I am looking forward to knocking out all the samurai!"

Ignoring the young pretentious man, Kenji bows to you. He is instantaneously imitated by all the other samurai. You bow to them before inviting the twins to do the same. You then start walking towards Mount Fuji, and motion to the twins to follow you.

Walk to section 79

74

"I'm sorry," you tell Raju and Sunita, "but I don't feel comfortable stealing a treasure."

"Stealing?" says Raju. "We would not steal anything! It's an abandoned fortune, that's all! It's just sitting there, so why not take it before someone else does?"

"Simply because it's not ours," you calmly say. "I don't want to take part of this."

"But we need your help to find it!" continues Raju. "You are so smart, have amazing skills, and we can really use your help to navigate through the enormous Pyramid of the Sun!"

"I'm sorry," you simply say.

You turn your back to Raju in order to pick up some more pink moss...

...big mistake...

In a moment of rage, Raju delivers a powerful and vicious kick to the back of your head. You die instantly, since the ruthless blow ruptures your spinal cord at the neck, sending you permanently to the spirit world.

In a few days, Manna's granddaughter Shirisha will join you in the afterlife...since you never brought her any pink moss to heal her infection.

Did you forget never to turn your back on a potential opponent? Well, it doesn't matter anymore because for you it is.

THE END

75

Staring at the brave warriors facing you, you finally tell Kenji:

"The eleventh samurai is the highest ranking warrior here today."

Looking up at the sky, Kenji simply says to you:

"You were not able to see nor listen to the obvious, Cho-san."

All of a sudden, an arrow is fired your way, but your incredibly fast hand catches it in mid-air before it hits you! You throw it in front of you, and tell Kenji:

"No one has the power to insult you if you don't let their words bother you."

Suddenly, a black poisoned arrow hits you deeply between the shoulder blades.

"THE NINJAS ARE ATTACKING!" yells Sawato. "REGROUP!"

You feel the deadly poison enter your blood stream as Sunita runs up to you to help. Regrettably, there is nothing she can do for you.

THE END

76

Still in its beautiful sheath, Kenji takes his long sword, and gives it to you.

"Cho-san, please accept this *katana* sword as a small token on my infinite gratitude. You have earned it."

You look at the beautiful sword and smile. Not to offend Kenji, you tell him:

"Thank you Kenji-san for such an honorable gift. But...I am not worthy of it."

"You saved my life, Cho-san. My friends and I are honored by your presence. The gift of a sword for a life is the least I can do."

All the other samurai walk up to you, and bow to you. Very respectfully, with the outmost courtesy, you do the same.

Now reach section 73

77

Your fabulous sixth sense tells you to immediately accept Raju's offer...for now! You sense a great danger nearby, and feel that accepting his offer could even save your life!

Get ready for section 82...

78

You slowly open your eyes and your gaze fixes the ceiling. You feel your back pressing against the comfortable hotel room mattress, and your hand still holding onto the pink moss. You carefully get up before giving your body a good stretch. You look at your watch: it's 9:00pm.

"Wow! Time really flies inside the akashic records' time capsules. I thought I was gone for maybe one hour. I still have time to see Manna. But how do I call for her?"

You sit on the edge of the bed, feeling the softness and texture of the *shibazakura*. Spontaneously, you lift your head up, and say in a very delicate voice:

"Manna...I am back in my hotel room...I have the rare healing pink moss for your granddaughter..."

A few seconds later, Manna appears in front of you with a majestic smile on her lovely face. She approaches you, and says as she takes your hand:

"Welcome back, *Chosen One*. I knew I could count on you."

"I really want your granddaughter to heal."

"I know, my dear. You are such a good hearted person. How was your first trip inside a time capsule?"

"It was very...adventurous...to say the least. Above all I met the twins Sunita and Raju. He is quite a character, and she is more soft spoken."

"Well, I am glad you are back in one piece. Those trips can be sometimes dangerous."

"Yes they can."

"Forgive me, but I must get back at once, and prepare the special ointment for Shirisha. Would you like to join me to see her? She is not sleeping right now."

"It would be my pleasure."

Putting one hand on your forehead, Manna says:

"Just close your eyes, my dear, and let me do everything."

You close your eyes, and feel a delicate energy flowing from Manna's hand to your forehead. A few seconds later, you feel as if your body was starting to float on a soft cloud, rocking you back and forth, like a gentle sea. All sorts of pleasant images appear in your head. A moment later, you are standing inside Shirisha's bedroom with Manna by your side. The teenage girl is lying in bed, obviously suffering a lot. Her long black hair is tied in a bun, to uncover her forehead drenched in sweat caused by her high fever. She is uncontrollably trembling under her blanket. Nevertheless, she finds the strength to send you a gracious smile.

"Shirisha, you have a special visitor...this is *The Chosen One!*"

The young girl tries to sit up on her bed, but you motion for her not to try.

"Please keep your strength," you tell her. "I brought you some *shibazakura*. This rare pink moss will cure you."

She looks at you, takes your hand, and smiles again.

"Thank you, *Chosen One*. Thank you."

"I will now let you rest. Sweet dreams Shirisha. I will come back in a few days, when you feel better."

You smile at her, and turn to Manna. She is staring at you with tears in her eyes, feeling overwhelmed with joy, and human love. She approaches you, and gives you a big hug.

"You saved my little girl, *Chosen One*. Thanks to you, she will live."

"Yes she will. Do you need my help to prepare the ointment?"

"No thank you, *Chosen One*. I sense you have a big day tomorrow. Be careful my dear, and remember to use all the skills that you have. "

"I will be careful."

"As soon as you are ready to take the twins to see Gutuk, call upon me wherever you are. I will then appear and help you."

"Thank you Manna."

"Goodbye for now."

Once again, you close your eyes, and feel a delicate energy flowing from Manna's hand to your forehead. You then feel your body floating onto a soft invisible cloud, being gently rocked as pleasant images appear in your head. A moment later, you are back in your hotel room, lying on your bed. You get up and look at the time.

"It's already 9:20pm. I'm too tired to eat, and I'm not hungry anyway. I should go to bed."

You take a quick shower, brush your teeth, and go to bed. You close your eyes, and quickly fall asleep.

Sweet dreams. Wake up at section 86

79

Raju runs up to you and says:

"Hey Cho, why do you want us to follow you?"

"I am doing you a favor," you simply reply. "You want to stay alive? Stay away from the samurai."

"Why is that?"

"Your rudeness and disrespect got under their skin, and made their blood boil. Hence, they don't like you very much."

"I'm not afraid of them."

"You should be."

Sunita gently grabs you by the arm which brings you to a halt.

"By the way, thank you Cho. Thank you for saving my brother. Why did you do it?"

"He would have now been dead otherwise..."

"But YOU could have gotten killed! You risked your life for a perfect stranger!!" continues Sunita.

"I have to say...what you did for me was really cool! Thanks!" adds Raju.

"Don't mention it," you reply.

You reach the bottom on Mount Fuji, and start collecting the pink moss, thinking about Shirisha and her grandmother. Sunita starts to help you collect the *shibazakura* but Raju simply stands there, lost in his thoughts. Finally he says:

"Listen Cho, deep down inside I'm a good guy. I appreciate what you have done for me. Let me thank you my way."

"I'm listening."

"Tomorrow, me and my sister are planning to enter another time capsule. We want to travel to Guatemala in the year 750 AD."

"Why do you want to do that?"

"I will explain," says Sunita. "In history, there used to be a city in northern Guatemala, built by the Maya, named Tikal. It was built inside a massive green forest. Then, in 732 AD, the Maya people built an impressive temple: the *Tikal Temple 1*, also called *the Temple of the Great Jaguar*. According to an ancient legend from the Valley of Mexico, the Maya wanted to protect and safeguard an unbelievable treasure they were keeping in that temple. They decided to hide their astonishing fortune somewhere inside the Pyramid of the Sun located in Teotihuacan city."

"Where is Teotihuacan city?" you asked intrigued.

"It's in the Valley of Mexico, about 48 kilometers or 30 miles northeast of Mexico city," continues Sunita.

"How big is this Pyramid?"

"It's huge: 220 meters or 720 feet in length, and about 70 meters or 220 feet in height! The legend says that the treasure is hidden somewhere inside, behind a massive bronze door. Only a unique golden key can open it. Guess where that key is?"

"Somewhere inside the Temple of the Great Jaguar!" says Raju with excitement. "We must find the golden key in order to find the immense treasure. So first, we will travel to Guatemala in the year 732 AD, and then to the Pyramid of the Sun. We will share the fortune with you once we find it. What do you say, Cho?"

If you refuse Raju's proposition, run to section 74

If you accept it, get ready for section 82

If you master the sixth sense, check out section 77

80

With great attention, you look at all eleven samurai standing before you. After a long pause, you finally proclaim:

"The highest ranking samurai is the second one."

Kenji stares at you with a disappointed look in his eyes:

"It is the wrong answer, Cho-san..."

Sawato fires a deadly arrow your way, but you intercept it in mid-air...thanks to your amazing reflexes. You jam the arrow into the soil at your feet, and say:

"I think we are done here."

Out of the blue, a meter-long poisoned arrow pierces your flesh from the back, and lodges itself deeply into your spine.

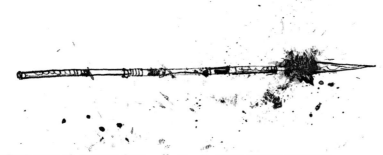

"THE NINJAS ARE BACK!" yells Kenji. "WE MUST FIGHT!"

You collapse to the ground, slowly losing consciousness. It's very sad that your mission is over.

THE END

81

Since you decided to go left, you all quickly reach the end of the narrow hallway. There is nothing more than a thick wall in front of you, built with heavy square stone plates.

"Great!" says Raju. "What now?"

As you look down at your feet, you notice a stone plate sticking out of the wall. Spontaneously, you crouch and apply a pressure on it with both hands. Out of the blue, a big stone block falls right onto your head, taking your life...

Your mission is over, but it's not your fault. Accidents do happen, but sometimes we end up paying a heavy price for them. In your case, your death signifies the end of our world as we know it. Soon, Raju and Sunita will start altering the present and the future. How? By changing past events, and eliminating people they don't like from the akashic records' time capsules.

Why did you have to push that stone?

THE END

82

"*For me to eventually bring these twins to Gutuk - the gate keeper of time - they must first learn to trust me. Thus, I must spend as much time as I can with them until I find the right moment to neutralize them,*" you think to yourself. "*Whatever we now change in history will later be changed back by Gutuk. This way no harm will be done.*"

"I accept your offer," you tell the twins.

"Of course you do!" says Raju.

"What about the martial arts tournaments?" you ask.

"What about it!?" responds Raju rudely. "Did you forget that we are inside the akashic records? We can jump to any time capsule at any moment. Kenji...I mean Kenji-san...said the tournament is only next week, but we could go now, if we wanted to, by travelling to its specific time capsule. How cool is that!"

"You are right brother!" says Sunita.

"I now have to go back to Kathmandu to deliver this pink moss," you tell the twins.

"You do that," says Raju bluntly.

You look at the obnoxious young man, and say:

"You know, if you need my help so badly in your treasure quest, the least you can do is to be polite, and to address me with respect."

"I agree," says Sunita.

"All right, all right," blabs the teenager.

"Our adventure starts tomorrow," continues Sunita. "I suggest we all leave the physical world on Earth at 9:00am to meet

in Guatemala, in front of the *Temple of the Great Jaguar*."

"Good idea," you respond. After quickly taking some more *shibazakura*, you tell the twins:

"I will see you tomorrow."

You smile before disappearing before their eyes. A moment later, they disappear as well.

Continue your journey at section 78

83

You approach the left door, and grab the knob. It easily turns in your hand. You gently push the door, and step into nothing more than a completely empty room! The floor and walls are made of large grey limestone plates, and there is a heavy moldy smell in the air. In the wall to your right, you see two more doors. You open them, and step back into the initial stone hallway you just came from.

"This is strange. All three doors lead to the same empty room," you tell Sunita.

"Why would anyone install three doors, one next to the other, which lead into the same room?" she asks.

"I don't care," blurs out Raju.

"Let's just continue," you tell the twins.

Follow the torches to section 94

84

Straight away, your eyes come across the majestic kapok trees of the Maya forest all around you. It is so green and vibrant that it appears to be tainted with a bright aura. The pure air is perfumed with a delicate scent from the bitter orange trees. Surrounding you, people are walking by, conversing very pleasantly with one another, going about their usual business. In front of you, the impressive Temple of the Great Jaguar seems to be waiting for you with its thick stairs built in heavy stones. You look up, and notice the twins already waiting for you.

"The adventure continues," you tell yourself.

Taking your time, you walk up the stairs, enjoying the magnificent view.

"Good morning," you tell the sister and brother.

"Good afternoon you mean," says Raju. "You see Cho, the sun is already very high in the sky."

"Yes it is. How are you Sunita?"

"I'm so excited! I can't wait to find that golden key, and then the treasure!"

"Let's not waste any more time. Let's just go Sunita," says the teenage boy.

You all turn around, and step inside the temple. After just a few steps, you see a wall in front of you but you have the option of going left or right. Either way seems safe since you see the end of a very short stone hallway in both directions.

"Where do you wish to go?" you ask the twins.

"You decide," says Raju. "After all, you are the smart one."

If you wish to turn right, walk to section 87

If you wish to go left, reach section 81

85

"I must guess correctly...or else..."

You bend down to grab a big rock. As you hold it in your hand, you look at all the brave samurai standing before you, wondering which one is the highest ranking warrior. After a very long moment, you say:

"I know who it is. It is the fourth samurai to my left."

"I am very sorry," replies Kenji.

Sawato shoots a deadly arrow your way, but you instinctively place the rock you are holding on your chest. The arrow crashes on the rock, and breaks into pieces. You walk up to Kenji, and say:

"It's time to move on to something more constructive than this..."

Abruptly, you fall flat onto your stomach with a poisoned arrow lodged in your back.

"NINJAS!" yells Kenji.

You close your eyes...and stop breathing.

THE END

86

You wake up at 8:00am the next morning, feeling refreshed but very hungry. You get up, freshen up, and quickly get dressed.

"I forgot that last time I ate was twenty-four hours ago!"

You leave your room, and go straight to the eating area. As you walk in, you notice many set tables in the middle of the room.

"Good morning, says an older waitress dressed in a traditional Nepalese dress. Please help yourself to our complimentary Himalayan buffet."

"Thank you. What a nice surprise!"

You walk up to the tables and see delicious freshly made omelets, steamy pancakes and waffles, a mountain of fresh fruits, freshly made breads, various cold cuts, local pastries, and many more delights.

"Let's try a little bit of everything," you tell yourself.

You take a brass plate, and help yourself to all this mouth-watering food. A moment later, you sit down at a nearby table, and let your taste buds do the rest.

"Simply scrumptious," you think to yourself.

A little while later, after eating, you are enjoying a large glass of freshly squeezed orange juice. Looking at your watch, you then realize it's already

8:55am.

"Time to go meet the twins."

Feeling very satisfied with your meal, you get up and walk back to your room. You lock the door behind you, lie down on your bed, and start relaxing your body.

"I wish to find myself in Guatemala, in the year 732 AD, in front of the Temple of the Great Jaguar."

Focusing on the infinite energy flowing through your body, you close your eyes. While breathing very deeply and slowly, you repeat your final destination in your head. You start accelerating the movement of your body's molecules. Within seconds your molecules are moving so fast that your body becomes transparent...and finally disappears. You feel your entire being fly higher and higher, as you enter a gargantuan tunnel of marvelous white light. Your body is propelled forward at tremendous speed as you reach the splendid spirit world. In your head, you once again repeat the words *Temple of the Great Jaguar*. A moment later, you are standing in front of it, in Guatemala...

It is time to reach section 84

87

As you turn right, you reach the end of the narrow hallway in just a few steps. In front of you, there is only a thick wall built with square stone plates.

"So what are we supposed to do now?" complains Raju.

"Think and stop whining all the time," Sunita tells him.

You turn around, and press your back against the wall to analyze the current situation. All of a sudden, an enormous stone plate starts to move under your feet. You jump high off it, as the plate slides into the lower wall, leaving a big square hole behind which appears to be an entrance of some sort.

"A secret passage!" says Sunita. "Cho, you are a genius!"

To your great surprise, there is light

coming from inside the passage. As you approach it, you see a solid wooden ladder fixed to the back wall.

"Go first Cho. I'm a little scared," says Sunita.

"I'M NOT!" yells her silly brother.

"Not so loud," you tell the teenager. Grabbing onto the ladder, you carefully start going down the passage with the twins following you behind. About a minute later, you finally reach the bottom of the temple. You take a few steps down another stone hallway, and say to the twins:

"The only light we have is coming from burning torches fixed to the stone walls. I wonder who takes care of lighting them..."

"Who cares! It's probably somebody with no job!" replies Raju. "Let's find that golden key."

"Raju stop your rudeness!" says Sunita.

You walk forward, feeling very fortunate for having the torches light your way. A few seconds later, you notice three thick wooden doors to your right. They all look the same, and there is nothing particular about them. Nevertheless, you stop, and stare at the doors.

If you want to try to open the left door, go ahead in section 83

If you prefer to try to open the middle door, try your luck in section 91

If you wish to try to open the right door, push it in section 97

If you master the sixth sense, check out section 89

If you don't want to open any of the doors, continue walking to section 94

88

"Let's try the fluorescent yellow pole," you tell the twins.

You grab onto the pole and, followed by Sunita and Raju, you let yourself go down. You all slide in total darkness for a minute...than five...than twenty...

"Oh no!" you tell yourself, understanding too late what is happening...

You see, a dark magical spell has been caste on this pole in order to protect the golden key from eventual thieves. You will all continue sliding down for eternity...that is until your hearts stop beating. The twins have definitively been neutralized...but what does it matter if you are dead?

THE END

89

Your outstanding sixth sense does not detect any danger behind these doors. As a matter of fact, it fills you with a bizarre feeling of...emptiness!

If you want try to open the left door, go ahead in section 83

If you prefer to try to open the middle door, try your luck in section 91

If you wish to open the right door, pull it at section 97

If you don't want to open any of the doors, continue walking to section 94

90

You focus on all the samurai, not knowing which one to pick. Finally, you tell Kenji:

"The highest ranking samurai is the ninth man in front of me."

With a very sad face, Kenji tells you:

"It's not the ninth man, Cho-san."

An arrow is fired your way, but you catch it in mid-air before it pierces your chest. You throw it back to Sawato, and say out loud:

"People can't move forward if their ego gets in the way."

 Unexpectedly, a poisoned shuriken hits you in the back.

"THE NINJAS ARE BACK!" yells a samurai. "TAKE OUT YOUR WEAPONS!"

This time, there is no way out for you. In a few seconds, you will be gone...

THE END

91

You grab the middle door's knob, and it easily turns in your hand. You push the door, and step into a completely empty room! The floor and walls are made of large grey limestone blocks, and there is a heavy moldy smell in the air. Next to the door you just opened, you see two more doors. You open both doors, and step into the initial stone hallway you just came from.

"I don't understand this," says Sunita. "All three doors lead to the same smelly room."

"Someone installed three doors...one next to another...which all lead to the same room. That's interesting...to say the least," you tell the teenage girl.

"No it's not," yaps back Raju.

"Time to continue our journey," you tell the twins.

Leave this room and go to section 94

92

"Let's go down the blue pole," you say out loud.

You grab onto the pole and let yourself go down. You hear Sunita and Raju, complaining about how dark it is, as they are sliding down just above your head. Brusquely, the pole ends! You all have nowhere to go but down...swallowed by the total darkness. You free fall for about a minute before crashing into the hard ground. You all die instantly, but painlessly.

The twins have been stopped...but only accidently. As for you, you will be greatly missed by all your loved ones. It's unfortunate that your mission has to end this way.

THE END

93

You decide to walk up to the door numbered four. You open it, and step inside. Surprisingly, you find yourself in a room exactly the same size as the previous one, but this one is covered with thick wooden boards everywhere! You slowly walk around the room, asking yourself why anyone would build a room like this one inside a majestic temple. Wondering the same thing, the twins follow you. Suddenly, you all hear a loud and powerful voice, proclaiming:

"HURRY...OR THE GOLDEN KEY WILL BE LOST FOREVER!"

In one corner of the room, you notice two doors. You quickly run up to them, and see six dots on one door, and seven on the other. Time is running out!

If you want to open door number seven, hurry to section 102

**If door number six is the one you want to open,
don't waste time and run to section 107**

94

You keep walking straight ahead, followed by Sunita and the cranky Raju.

"It's so humid in here," says Sunita. "It smells very bad."

"We're not here to smell the air but to find a golden key!" replies Raju.

"Oh be quiet!" barks back Sunita.

"Being around these two is more exhausting than dealing with this strong smell," you tell yourself. *"They behave like little kids!"*

The stone hallway abruptly branches off to the left. Right around the corner, the hallway suddenly ends and you notice six large rectangular openings cut right into the stone wall. In each opening, there is a vertical metal pole, similar to a firefighter's sliding pole. They appear to be connecting the floor you are on to somewhere below. Strangely, each pole is covered with a bright fluorescent colour!

"This is incredible!" you say out loud. "Who designed these...and where do these poles lead to?"

"TO THE GOLDEN KEY!" yells Raju.

"There is only one way to find out..." you tell the obnoxious teenager.

"Are you ready to slide down, sister?" asks Raju.

If you want to slide down the fluorescent yellow pole, go ahead at section 88

If you prefer to go down the fluorescent orange pole, check out section 99

If you choose the fluorescent blue pole, get ready for section 92

If you want to grab onto the fluorescent green pole, good luck in section 96

If you pick the fluorescent red pole, enjoy sliding to section 106

If you feel like going down the fluorescent purple pole, grab onto it in section 101

95

For a long time you stare at all eleven warriors facing you, trying to feel who is the highest ranking samurai. You finally say:

"I have the answer: the highest ranking samurai is the seventh one."

With great sadness in his eyes, Kenji replies: "No...he is not."

An arrow is instantaneously fired towards your chest, but you catch it in mid-air before it reaches you. You break it against your knee, and throw it behind you:

"Kenji-san, I don't deserve to die...and you know it!"

Without any warning, a poisoned arrow hits you between the shoulder blades.

"NINJAS ARE ATTACKING US ONCE AGAIN!" yells Sawato. "FIGHT!"

You fall onto your stomach, realizing that for you, it is...

THE END

96

You walk up to the green pole, and say:

"Since the colour green represents good health, I choose this pole."

"It also sometimes represents banknotes...lots of them!" says Raju.

Ignoring him, you let yourself slide down the pole, followed by the twins. About ten seconds later, you land in the middle of an empty large room built entirely of grey limestone blocks.

"What is this place?" asks Raju.

"It's a room made of stone blocks," answers his sister.

"You think?" replies the arrogant young man.

"It's actually limestone," you tell the twins. "That's what the Maya used as building material."

You then notice four wooden doors, one in each corner of the room. You rapidly walk up closer to every door, observing that each one is engraved with a different symbol. The twins quickly join you in your observation.

"What have you found?" asks Sunita.

"Four doors," says Raju. "Doors with dots."

You look at him, and calmly explain:

"This door, in front of us, is engraved with one dot. It is based on the Maya numerical system. Basically, it is how the Maya people wrote down numbers. It means we are facing door number one."

"So the door engraved with two dots would be door number two," states Sunita.

"Correct," you tell the young lady.

"Boring," mumbles Raju.

Ignoring once again the young man's rudeness, you address Sunita:

"It's time to continue our journey."

"So where do we go now?" she asks. "Which door do we open?"

If you choose to open the door with four dots, step into section 93

If you wish to open the door with two dots, go ahead in section 108

If you prefer going for the door with three dots, open it in section 98

If the door with one dot is your choice, grab its door knob in section 103

If you master the sixth sense skill and want to use it, check out section 111

97

You open the right door, and step into an empty room! The floor and walls are made of large grey limestone blocks, and there is a moldy smell in the air. Next to the door you just opened, you see two more doors. You open them, and step out into the same stone hallway you just came from.

"All three doors lead to this same empty, smelly room," says Sunita. "Why?"

"Who cares!" barks Raju. "Someone must love doors."

"Why would someone install three doors, one next to the other, to get inside the same room?" continues his sister.

"I have better things to worry about," replies Raju.

"Alright...let's continue," you tell the twins.

Follow the torches along the wall to section 94

98

Followed by the twins, you step inside an empty room entirely covered in ice! In the middle of the room, you notice two larges openings in the floor. Above these openings, hanging from the ceiling, you see two long ropes which lead into the openings. One rope is very thick, and the other one is much thinner. They appear to be leading very deep inside the openings.

Unexpectedly, you all hear a loud and powerful voice, saying:

"YOU WANT THE GOLDEN KEY? THEN FIND IT BEFORE IT IS LOST FOREVER!"

"WE MUST HURRY!" yells Raju. "COME ON!!"

It's time for some exercise:

Go down the thick rope and you will end up in section 104...

If the thinner rope is for you, let yourself go down to section 115

99

"Let's go down the fluorescent orange pole," you tell the eager sister and her brother.

"I hate the colour orange," says Raju.

You grab onto the pole and, followed by both teenagers, you let yourself go down. Sliding in total darkness, you gradually start to feel more and more dizzy.

"What is happening to me?" you tell yourself. *"It's suddenly getting*

harder and harder to breathe."

"CHO!" screams Sunita. "I CAN BARELY BREATHE!"

You realize that there is less and less oxygen as you slide down the pole. The faster your slide down...the less oxygen you get.

"TRY TO STOP SLIDING. WE MUST TRY TO PULL OURSELVES BACK UP!" you yell to the siblings.

But it's too late. Both sister and brother lose consciousness, and fall on you. The shock makes you drop the pole, and you all fall together into the darkness. In a moment, you will all crash against enormous rocks. For you, the evil twins, and your mission, it is...

THE END

100

You approach the samurai, then move back again, studying the way they look at you, and react to you.

"I feel the highest ranking samurai is the sixth one, Kenji-san."

He looks straight into your eyes, and says:

"Your feeling is wrong, Cho-san."

Sawato shoots an arrow right at your chest, but you catch it with an incredibly fast movement of your hand.

"Brave samurai," you tell the group, "words can only hurt you if you let them. Forgive this young man..."

You don't get to finish your sentence because a poisoned arrow suddenly hits you from the back, and lodges itself deep into your spine.

"I SEE NINJAS!" yells Kenji. "SWORDS OUT!"

You would have loved to join forces with the samurai, but you are already dead.

THE END

101

"I love the colour purple," says Raju. "It's the colour of the bruises I gave some students at school...Ha! Ha! Ha!"

"You're such a bully Raju!" replies Sunita.

"Let's see where this pole leads to..." you tell yourself.

You slide down the pole, and land back on your feet a few seconds later. To your astonishment, you find yourself in the middle of a room with walls covered with gold! You slowly walk around, not understanding where you are...

"What is this place?" you ask yourself. *"A room with golden walls? This makes no sense."*

"HURRAY!" screams Sunita. "WE ARE SO RICH!!!"

"We are already filthy rich sister," brags Raju. "What's your point?"

"Don't celebrate just yet," you tell the young woman.

As you say these words, the entire room's floor collapses, sending you all into complete darkness! You were right not to rejoice so quickly. You will soon crash against the ground...and there is nothing you can do about it...

THE END

102

As you swing door number seven open, you immediately step inside a very large square room. Its floor, walls, and ceiling are covered with lime mortar encrusted with thousands of tiny diamonds!

"WOW! DIAMONDS!" screams Sunita. "I LOVE DIAMONDS! LET'S PICK SOME OUT!!"

"Hold on," you tell the smitten girl. "Let's focus on finding the golden key."

"But Cho..." says Sunita.

"We are here for the key. Let's not get distracted. Look you two: there are six doors right in front of us. This means we have to keep going."

"You're no fun, Cho," mutters Raju.

Frustrated with your decision, Sunita walks away very quickly towards the six doors. She abruptly stops, and says:

"I can't believe it! Each one of these doors is made out of a different precious metal from the platinum group: ruthenium, rhodium, palladium, osmium, iridium, and platinum itself. Each door is worth a fortune!"

"How do you know so much about these precious metals?" you enquire, impressed.

"They are used in art and fine jewelry making…and I love jewelry!"

"I see," you simply answer.

"My sister really knows her jewelry…I give her that!"

"I'm sure she does, but we have to move forward," you quickly say to get back on track.

As you say these words, a very alarming feeling wraps itself around you, as if someone was watching your every move, waiting for the right moment to strike…

If you want to open the ruthenium door, step into section 109

If the rhodium door is your choice, open it in section 118

If you prefer opening the door made of palladium, go ahead in section 114

How about the platinum door? Run to section 125 to open it

If the osmium door appeals the most to you, get ready for section 121

If you master the sixth sense, take a peek at section 116

If you choose the door made of iridium, hurry to section 129

103

You slowly open the one doted door. Followed by Sunita and her brother, you step inside a tiny room almost the size of a closet! The floor, walls and ceiling are totally covered with tiny white pebbles. At your feet, you notice three openings in the floor, dogged one next to the other. A violent heat coming out of the middle opening suddenly hits you in the face. You look inside…and see a large river of burning lava flowing very fast!

Without prior notice, you all hear a loud and powerful voice, announce:

"YOU WANT TO FIND THE GOLDEN KEY? THEN JUMP INTO THE CORRECT OPENING… OR IT WILL BE LOST… FOREVER!"

"Hey! Let's jump into the lava and see what happens!" says Raju.

"Very funny," replies Sunita. "What do you think Cho? Should we jump at all? Is this the only way to find the golden key?"

"Something tells me that there is no other way," you answer her.

**If you wish to jump into the left side opening,
jump for your life into section 113**

**By jumping into the right side opening,
you will find yourself in section 117...**

...so choose wisely!

104

As you go down the thick rope, a very powerful wind suddenly grips all of you...out of nowhere! It brusquely starts to violently shake the rope in every direction!

"WHAT IS HAPPENING?!" screams Sunita.

"BE QUIET!" replies Raju.

"HANG ON TIGHT!" you yell out to the twins.

But a vicious gust of wind rips the thick rope out of your hands! A second later, you are all falling into the bloodcurdling darkness...

Prepare yourself for section 119!

105

Your phenomenal sixth sense tells you that you are being asked a trick question. The answer which you are being led to provide is misleading, and completely different from the right one!

If you choose:

the eleventh samurai, choose section 75

the tenth samurai, prepare yourself for section 55

the third samurai, sneak up to section 65

the ninth samurai, simply go to section 90

the eight samurai, run to section 70

the first samurai to your left, good luck at section 50

to clarify the meaning of friendship, do so at section 110

the seventh samurai, turn to section 95

the second samurai, discover section 80

the fourth samurai, get ready for section 85

the fifth samurai, walk to section 60

the sixth samurai, run to section 100

106

"I would like to go down the red pole," says Sunita.

"I was just about to suggest that," you tell her. "Go ahead, you lead the way."

"I'm a little scared. I prefer to follow you, Cho."

You grab onto the red pole and let yourself slide down, followed by Sunita and her brother.

"IT'S SO DARK IN HERE!" yells Raju. "I HATE IT!"

You pick up speed when out of nowhere, the pole breaks! You all fall into the unknown, swallowed by the unforgiving darkness. What you don't know yet...

...is that you will free fall forever...

...but your body will not survive this long.

THE END

107

You open the door with the six dots on it and step inside. To your absolute dismay, you find yourself in a wild jungle! Its trees are massive and very tall; colourful birds are flying above your head; cute fury animals are walking around everywhere, and feasting on berries...

"What in the world is this place?" asks Sunita. "It looks like a real jungle!"

"It is a jungle, sister," replies sarcastically Raju. "You are very observant."

"Oh quiet!" she says with an irritated voice.

To your left, you see a tree even bigger than the others. Its thick branches are growing in all possible directions, but it has no leaves at all! In the trees' trunk, you notice a large door engraved with one dot. Suddenly, you hear a very delicate voice fill the air, and whisper:

"OPEN THIS DOOR...AND FIND THE GOLDEN KEY..."

"Well what are we waiting for?" asks Raju. "LET'S GO GET THAT KEY!"

"Don't rush," you calmly tell the excited teenager. "Let's be careful and take our time."

Go to section 103

108

You open door numbered two, and walk into a cold room. The walls, floor, and ceiling are all built with limestone blocks, and there is a strong moldy smell in the air. In one of the room's corners, you see two wooden doors. One of the doors has a single horizontal short line engraved on it. The other door is more robust, and has two short horizontal white lines: one line is painted underneath the other.

"What do these lines mean?" asks Sunita.

"It means someone has nothing better to do than to paint or engrave

white lines on doors," grunts Raju.

"In the Maya numeric system, one short horizontal line represents the number five while two lines - one underneath the other - represent the number ten."

"How exciting...not!" says Raju. "Where do we go now?"

Out of nowhere, you all hear a loud and powerful voice, proclaim:

"THE GOLDEN KEY WILL BE LOST FOREVER...IF YOU DON'T HURRY!"

"What was that?" asks Raju.

"Cho! What do we do?!" says Sunita.

It's your call...you can open door number five at section 120...

....or if you choose door number ten, quickly go to section 112

109

Before you are able to put your hand on its square handle, the ruthenium door magically opens by itself! You cautiously step inside the room, and simply cannot believe your eyes. The immense hexagonal room before you is filled with thousands of shiny gold coins! Along the walls, an absurd quantity of stacked gold coins reaches all the way to the ceiling, covering every wall, as well as the floor. Anywhere you look, there are massive piles of gold coins spilling everywhere...The twins just stand agape behind you, speechless...

"I can barely breathe when I look at all this gold," murmurs Sunita.

"Me too," mumbles Raju, mesmerized by such an unbelievable fortune before him.

"We have to take all this gold with us," continues the infatuated girl.

"Absolutely!" proclaims her brother.

In the middle of the hexagonal room, you notice a shiny object simply floating in the air! You slowly approach it...and realize it is a beautifully crafted golden key! It is slowly turning on itself...just like planet Earth rotates on its axis. You get closer to it, and observe it with fascination.

"WE FOUND THE GOLDEN KEY!" yells Raju.

He eagerly rushes towards the key before grabbing it! Out of the blue, everything in the room immediately disappears, leaving you and the twins in total darkness!

"CHO! WHAT IS HAPPENING?!" panics Sunita. Only then, gargantuan flames unexpectedly appear all around you, circling all of you, as a threatening voice proclaims very loudly:

"THE GOLDEN KEY IS DESTINED ONLY FOR THOSE WITH A PURE

HEART. YOURS IS NOT, YOUNG MAN. BY TOUCHING THE GOLDEN KEY, YOU ARE NOW CURSED...AND SO IS EVERYONE WITH YOU."

The burning flames rapidly close up on you...and there is nowhere to escape. You attempt to visualize leaving this time capsule in order to find Gutuk, but a superior power prevents you from doing so. Only then you understand that for you, it is...

THE END

110

"Kenji-san, you are asking me to tell you who is the highest ranking samurai amongst your friends?"

"That is correct, Cho-san."

"In other words, all of you, brave warriors, are mutual friends?"

"More like brothers," adds Kenji. "We would all die for one another."

You walk up to Kenji, feeling very relieved, and say:

"Kenji-san, there is no highest ranking samurai amongst all the warriors presently here. If there was, your traditions and etiquette would never allow you to call the highest ranking samurai a 'friend'. You would call him by his rank. That's my answer to your question."

Kenji looks at you in admiration, and for the first time, a big smile illuminates his face, softening his facial features.

"You are very clever, Cho-san. I am honored that you paid such close attention to my words."

INSTINCT! You turn around, and catch a long deadly flying arrow that was about to pierce you in the back. A second later, you catch another long flying arrow meant to enter Kenji's throat! Near the bottom of Fuji Mountain, you notice a dozen men, completely dressed in black, running in your direction.

"NINJAS!" yells Kenji. "PREPARE TO FIGHT!"

To your right, you hear Raju tell his sister:

"Sunita...I have the pink moss. Let's get out of here!"

"But Raju..."

"NOW!" he yells.

They both unexpectedly disappear, leaving you behind with all the samurai.

"*So much for their support!*" you tell yourself as you see the ninjas getting closer...

If you are a heavenly shield master,
now would be a good time to use it at section 42

If you want to fight the ninjas only using your martial art expertise,
good luck in section 57

If you can become a tornado and choose to do so,
transform yourself in section 43

If you master the skill of laser eyes, run to section 54

If you are an iron bolt master, you can use your skill in section 44

If you are able to paralyze your opponents, prepare for section 56

If you master the skill of ice bolt and feel like throwing a few,
cool the air in section 47

If you have the fire jet skill, heat things up in section 52

If you are able to fly, propel yourself to section 48

If you know how to become invisible, disappear in section 53

If you want to use your skill of telekinesis, watch out for section 49

If you are a telepathy master, jump inside section 51

111

"I don't feel any danger whatsoever behind these doors," you tell yourself. *"I can freely open whichever one I choose. But which one?"*

If you choose to open the door with four dots, step into section 93

If you wish to open the door with two dots, go ahead in section 108

If you prefer going for the door with three dots, open it in section 98

If the door with one dot is your choice, grab its knob in section 103

112

"Let's go through this one," you tell the twins.

You open the door...and find yourself at the edge of a marvelous sandy beach facing a splendid emerald coloured ocean! Its soft waves delicately wash up the shore, reaching a multitude of colourful seashells partially covered with golden sand. Pink flamingos are gliding through the turquoise sky above some spectacular dolphins propelling themselves out of the water, and back into the majestic white capped ocean.

"Wow!" says Sunita. "What a stunning place!! Let's go swimming!"

"Are you mad?" replies Raju. "We have a golden key to find, so keep your clothes on."

To your right, you see a cute little hut made entirely of straw. The entrance door is built with long solid bamboo strips, and a single green dot has been painted at the top of the door. Following your gut instinct, you tell the twins:

"We must go to that hut to see what's inside."

"Why?" says Raju. "That place looks like a dump."

"Oh stop being rude all the time!" tells him Sunita. "You are so unpleasant."

"I love you too sister," talks back the young man as he throws a seashell at her.

Walk in the soft sand to section 103

113

One after the other, you all jump into the lightless opening...and land into a deep dark pool of freezing water!

"Aaaaaahh!" What is this?" spontaneously yells Sunita. "I did not expect such a wet surprise since there is barely any light in this room, and I did not see where I was landing!"

"It's just very cold water," mocks her Raju.

You look around the dark room, and realize you are all swimming in some kind of giant wooden tub! You quickly swim to its edge, and pull yourself out. The twins immediately swim towards you, and you help them get out.

"Bbbbrrrrr! I'm so cold now!" says Sunita.

"We're all cold! Stop whining," replies a shivering Raju. "Don't be such a baby!"

"I'm sure there is an exit somewhere," you tell the twins. "Let's find it."

Followed by Sunita and her mouthy brother, you walk around the giant wooden tub, searching for an exit. A moment later, you say:

"There's our exit," as you point to a heavy metal door in one of the room's corners. "Let's go."

Continue your journey at section 98

114

"Let's try the palladium door," you tell the twins. "Who knows what's inside."

"Maybe the golden key!" says Raju.

He pushes you to the side, and yanks the door right open as he steps inside a tiny room. Unfortunately for him, he falls flat on his face...and stops breathing! A second later, Sunita and you collapse on the ground next to him...lifeless.

When he yanked the door to get inside the room, Raju triggered a deadly automatic mechanism. Thin arrows dipped in a very powerful poison were shot straight at whoever was standing in the doorway, including Sunita and you.

You tried your best.

THE END

115

You grab the thin rope, and gently let yourself slide down. Through the dark opening, you slowly enter a short vertical tunnel built with heavy limestones.

"It's cold and dark in here," says Sunita.

"Stop complaining," replies Raju.

Gradually, more light fills up the tunnel as you reach its bottom. The ground is cold but you notice many large torches fixed to the stone wall. The hot burning fire from the torches throws a warm orange light everywhere, illuminating a massive metal door, just in front of Sunita. You notice two blue dots painted on the door.

"I don't think we have a choice but to leave this tunnel through this door," you tell the siblings.

"At least there is a door," smiles Sunita.

"Who cares about the door! I want the golden key!" yaps Raju

Continue to section 108

116

You clear your mind, and let your eyes wander from door to door. Surprisingly, you can't activate your sixth sense at all! You are unable to feel which door to open...but you do sense an imminent danger threatening you.

"I don't understand," you tell yourself. *"I can't feel which way to go next! It's as if some superior power to my own was preventing me to use my magic. I have a bad feeling about this and must act quickly..."*

If you want to open:

the ruthenium door, step into section **109**

the rhodium door, open it in section **118**

the palladium door, go ahead in section **114**

the platinum door, run to section **125**

the osmium door, get ready for section **121**

the iridium door, hurry to section **129**

117

"See you down below," you tell Sunita and Raju as you jump into the right opening. Three seconds later, you land into a soft pile of sand. Immediately, you roll to the side so that the twins don't land on your head. You get back on your feet, and look around the strange room: it is shaped like a pentagon, and is entirely covered with sand.

"Impressive," Sunita tells you. She walks up to one of the walls before smelling it, and says:

"The sand covering this wall smells like eggs! YUK!!"

"I like eggs but only with bacon," mumbles Raju.

You look at Sunita and reply:

"Some people mix eggs with sand to get a more sturdy material. In other words, the sand mixed with eggs will become harder as it dries. I have even seen bridges built strictly with sand and eggs."

"Silly people," says Raju. "What a waste of eggs!"

Your gaze then notices a door covered with grayish sand right in front of you. It has two dots on it. You approach the door, followed by Raju and his sister.

"I don't see any other way out," you tell them. "Let's go."

Continue your journey at section 108

118

"Wait for me here," you tell the twins.

You open the rhodium door, and step inside a dark room where you can't see anything. All of a sudden, a very high pitch noise abruptly pierces your ears, and sends you to your knees. The unbearable pain pins you to the ground. You start to scream but it's too late. A second later, your body disappears into thin air, vaporized by an unknown magical power protecting this temple...

You will be greatly missed, and you will never find out what the twins will do next...

THE END

119

The ferocious wind keeps twirling you in every direction as you hear the teenagers' horrific screams! Images of your life flash before your eyes, as a sense of an imminent end wraps itself around you. Unexpectedly, an intense blinding white light makes you close your eyes, and you feel an odd heat starting to burn your face.

"WE'RE GONNA DIE!!!" yells Raju.

A moment later, the brutal wind abruptly stops blowing, the blinding white light disappears, and you stop falling! You open your eyes, and find yourself standing in a narrow stone hallway with four wooden doors. You see that they are all engraved with either one, two, three, or four dots.

"What was that crazy experience we just had?" asks Sunita.

"It's called falling into darkness while being shaken by a sadistic wind," says Raju.

You look at him, and calmly explain:

"This temple is protected by magical forces, so let's be ready for some more intense action. "

"Bring it on!" proclaims Raju.

"So, where do we go now?" whispers nervously Sunita.

If you choose to open the door with four dots, step into section 93

If you wish to open the door with two dots, go ahead in section 108

If you prefer going for the door with three dots, open it in section 98

If the door with one dot is your choice, grab its knob in section 103

If you master the sixth sense skill, check out section 111

120

You open the door with one horizontal line, and you all step inside...into total darkness! The large room you are all standing in is pitch black, and there is nothing to see...or almost. On the other side of where you are, you suddenly see two fluorescent doors appear. One is bright red, and the other one is electric yellow.

"This is a cool setting for Halloween," says Raju.

"You're so silly," replies his sister.

"Let's go towards these doors," you tell the twins.

You all walk up to the fluorescent doors, and inspect them from close. They seem to be lit from the inside, which gives out a powerful light.

"Cho, what do we do now?" asks Sunita.

If you want to open the bright red door, go to section 98

If you prefer opening the electric yellow door, do so at section 112

121

You pull the square osmium handle, but the door refuses to open. You try again with all your might, but the door won't budge.

"It's locked," you tell Sunita and Raju.

"Let me try," says the pretentious young man. Aggressively, he pulls the handle but the door stays closed. Raju tries again and again...with no results.

"Stop it," says Sunita. "We must try another door."

If you want to open the ruthenium door, step into section **109**

If the rhodium door is your choice, open it in section **118**

If you prefer opening the palladium, go ahead in section **114**

How about the platinum door? Run to section **125** to open it.

If you choose the iridium door, hurry to section **129**

122

"What an incredible ride this was!" tells you Sunita.

"It was indeed," you kindly answer.

"I hated it!!" babbles Raju. "Who was that silly 'king' anyway? He looked like a crazy Santa Claus with his bushy hair all tangled up in his filthy long beard. I'm sure there was a birds' nest hiding in there somewhere! He was obviously a master of magic...which makes him even more freaky!"

"Raju, why are you always so derogatory about everyone you see and everything you experience?" you ask the young man. "I don't remember you saying one positive thing about what you have experienced so far."

"That's just because you don't remember," yaps back Raju, trying to defend himself.

"Let's just go," takes over Sunita. "We have to get inside this pyramid. We are now standing at its base. So...should we go right or left?"

If you choose to go right,
follow the pyramid's base to section **131**

If you prefer to search the pyramid's base
by going left, walk to section **126**

123

You walk into the immense room...and are dumbfounded by what you see. Literally thousands of books are floating at eye level, moving in a circular motion around the room.

"WHAT IS THIS?" yells Raju. "FLYING BOOKS? THAT'S THE UNBELIEVABLE TREASURE KING FELIPE WAS TALKING ABOUT?"

"WHAT IS THE MEANING OF ALL OF THIS?" adds Sunita.

"I will tell you what is the meaning of all this," says a very pleasant and soothing voice.

You all turn around, and see a striking older woman sitting on a magnificent throne next to a handsome older man, also sitting on a similar majestic throne. They both stand up, and she says:

"I am Killa, Queen of the Pyramid of the Sun."

"...and I am King Beltak. This pyramid is our home."

"...and I'm Raju, a really exasperated guy who is sick of all this masquerade!!! Where is this absurd treasure we were told about?!"

The queen serenely looks at him. She gracefully walks towards the young man, in her spectacular green silk dress and dazzling golden crown. Queen Killa is immediately followed by her husband, King Beltak, a wide shouldered-man wearing an impeccable white and grey military uniform.

This king is almost dressed like Louis XVI, King of France, during the 1789 French Revolution, you think to yourself.

"Young man," the queen addresses Raju, "one of the greatest treasures you are looking for floats all around you: knowledge! With it, you can learn to take care of your health, provide for your loved ones, become wise and enlightened, learn how to travel and experience the world safely..."

"...learn about other cultures," continues the king, "master new languages, study philosophy, become a better person by discovering yourself even more..."

"WHAAAAAAT?" barks Raju.

"So we came here for that...for nothing?" says Sunita.

"Not for nothing," continues the queen. "You have discovered the importance of knowledge..."

"...and you have finally discovered us!" adds the king happily.

"What do you mean?" you ask King Beltak.

"My wife Queen Killa and myself have a story to tell you," replies the monarch.

"We don't have time for your boring stories!" yaps Raju.

You turn to the young man, and pierce him with your intense gaze. "Enough," you tell him. Precisely at that moment, you hear a loud pounding noise. It seems to be coming from inside the room you are in!

"What in the world was that?" asks the young pretentious teenager.

"We don't know for sure," replies the queen. "We often hear this noise, and it seems to be coming from inside the wall behind our thrones."

"We think it's the terrible *Beast*," adds the king.

"Beast?" you say. "What beast?"

As you let out those words, you hear once again a very loud pounding noise...coming from inside the back wall!

"I really must tell you our story," says King Beltak as the loud noise once again resonates in the entire room!

**If you wish to listen to the king,
make yourself comfortable at section 127**

**If you prefer to see where this strange and scary noise
is coming from, visit section 130**

124

"I pick the right tunnel," you tell the twins. "Let's go!"

You lay on your stomach and start crawling inside the very narrow tunnel. You have just enough room above your head to be able to look up towards the light. The tunnel is barely wider than your own body, forcing you to move very slowly.

"Cho!" says Sunita, "I feel a little claustrophobic in here!"

"You are doing great Sunita! You will be fine. Just keep following me."

"I hate this crazy place!" says Raju.

"Aaaaaaah!" screams Sunita.

"What's happening?" you ask her in a worried voice.

"There was this rectangular piece of stone or something sticking out of the left wall. I did not see it, and jammed my knee right against it. It just moved to the side, and at the same time it ripped my pants, giving me a bloody knee."

At that moment, a loud noise makes you stop crawling. A second later, you realize with horror that the side walls are starting to move towards you! The tunnel is quickly closing up on all of you. Sunita had accidently activated a deadly crank mechanism built inside the tunnel!!

"HURRY!" you tell the twins. "VISUALIZE THAT WE ARE BACK IN JAPAN!!"

"WHAT?" screams Raju.

But it's too late...and your mission has an abrupt crushing conclusion!

THE END

125

The platinum door opens easily, and you all walk into a very large hallway built out of jade plates from top to bottom! The warm green stone is superbly polished, and reflects an invisible omnipresent bright light around you.

"Where are we, Cho?" asks Sunita.

"In an annoying hallway," barks Raju.

After walking for a few minutes, you reach a massive jade door at the end of the hallway.

"What do we do now, Cho?" says the young woman.

"What do you think?" replies Raju. "Don't you see the door?"

"Shhhh!" says Sunita.

"Let's see where this leads to," you tell them.

Instinctively, you push the massive door, and it slowly opens. To your absolute dismay, you step into a very luxurious room that looks as if it was from the Italian Renaissance era. The hardwood floor is smooth, and runs across the entire room. Fabulous hand-made Persian rugs are slid under majestic walnut wardrobes placed along the back stone wall. Large impressionist paintings are elegantly hanging on the other side walls, delicately lit by the same invisible but omnipresent light.

Sitting on a colossal walnut chair covered with a thick red velvet padding, a very old man is smiling at you. His silky long hair is gently adorning his wrinkled face partially hidden by a long thick white beard. He is dressed like a king, and is holding a golden scepter. His sparkly blue eyes are fixing you with great admiration.

"I have been expecting you," says the old man. "I am King Felipe, and I am this country's monarch."

"You must do some serious renovations to this temple," dares to say Raju. "The nasty smell in some rooms..."

"Quiet Raju!" says Sunita.

Ignoring the young insolent, King Felipe continues:

"As you have noticed by now, many magical spells have been cast in this temple in order to protect it from thieves and intruders."

"Understandably," you reply.

"A few weeks ago, one of my wise sorcerers came to me. He said that a certain individual with a pure heart will come to my temple, looking the golden key..."

"I'm here!" says Raju. The king stands up, and slowly walks up to you, ignoring Raju.

"It is you," he proclaims. "You are the one I was waiting for...the one who will protect us from...certain villains." His gaze stops on Sunita and Raju.

"Cho, what is he talking about?" asks Sunita.

King Felipe graciously pulls out a small velvet box, and hands it to you.

"Open it," he tells you.

You open the velvet box...and discover a magnificently crafted golden key, inlayed with tiny rubies.

"This is what you came for, is it not?" says the king. "This key will open the door to ultimate wealth. You surely deserve it. This wealth is the secret to a successful and an abundant life. Make good use of it."

Looking at you deeply, he pauses for a moment, then continues:

"You must go to Teotihuacan city, in the valley of Mexico. There, you will find the Pyramid of the Sun. It is the largest structure in Teotihuacan city. You must walk around it in order to find a small square opening. It is the only passage which leads to the secret bronze door. The golden key will open it."

You then address the monarch: "Thank you so much for your help, King Felipe. How could I ever repay you?"

"Keep our world safe," answers the king. The old man's gaze dives straight into yours as he sends you this telepathic message:

"I know your true identity, *Chosen One*. My good friend Gutuk told me all about you, and your mission. That is why I am helping you stop these delusional and greedy teenagers. Beware: they are dangerous, especially Raju!"

It's time for section 135

126

You start walking along the pyramid's left side. Remembering King Felipe's advice, you are looking for one small square opening. You reach the pyramid's corner, and turn right. While walking along the pyramid's width, you closely observe every block that is forming the base...but you can't seem to find what you are looking for. In no time, you reach the pyramid's second corner, and turn right again. About half way through its length, you stop.

"I found it," you tell the twins, "...I mean...I found them!"

"What do you mean?" asks Sunita.

The twins simply become speechless for a moment when they see your discovery.

"Fantastic!" says Raju sarcastically. "There are two identical short square openings...cut through the solid rock...side-by-side! Which one are we supposed to choose now? Which one is the one we want?"

You look inside both openings, and realize you are facing two long tunnels.

"We will have to crawl inside one of these two tunnels. There is a little light coming from the end of each tunnel. This will help us."

If you want to crawl into the right tunnel,
get down on your stomach in section 124

If you choose to crawl inside the left one,
have fun at section 132!

127

"I would love to hear your story," you tell the monarch.

"But Cho...," starts Raju. You stop the reprehensible teenager with a simple gesture of your hand. The king and his queen slowly walk back to their thrones before comfortably sitting down. Queen Killa looks at you with a smile, and begins her story:

"Years ago, the Pyramid of the Sun was full of love, happiness, and wonderful people. Everyone was living in abundance, bliss, and mutual respect. One night, on his way back to our pyramid, my husband rescued a powerful young wizard named *Kesek* from a group of dangerous bandits. He invited the wizard to spend the night in our pyramid. The next morning, as a token of gratitude, Kesek cast a supernatural spell on both my husband's and my golden crown.

"What was the spell?" you ask intrigued.

"I am glad you ask," continues the king. "Kesek told us that from now on, both of our crowns would be magical. Each crown would grant two wishes per day to whomever would wear them!"

"Awesome!" yells Raju.

"But beware," adds the queen, "if a person would wish for something negative that could potentially create harm, that wish would not be granted, and the crown would simply vanish into thin air..."

"Unbelievable!" expresses Sunita.

"Years ago," continues King Beltak, "my father, King Melqiv, announced that the heir to the thrown will be me instead of my older brother Wexxer. My father thought that Wexxer was an immoral and self-centered man. When my brother heard my father's announcement, he became incredibly angry and jealous. You must know that my brother was also the apprentice of Tyrod, a selfish and dangerous sorcerer. Before my father died of very old age, Tyrod poured all his  knowledge of sorcery into Wexxer, who became a powerful sorcerer himself. In order to get revenge on my father, my brother cast powerful spells on the Pyramid of the Sun."

"What spells?" asks Sunita.

Queen Killa quickly glances at her, and answers:

"Wexxer made everyone and everything disappear from our pyramid, except for myself, my husband, and a few vestiges of our wealth. He made our pyramid seem abandoned, and transformed its many parts into death traps, in order for people to never find us. Wexxer magically trapped us inside this pyramid, not allowing us to leave this very room, and temporarily annihilating the power of our golden crowns. He had his personal servant bring us food and water. Day after day, Wexxer demanded that my husband give up his crown so he could become the new king. Wexxer's demand was in vain. One day, while napping outside in the warm sun, Wexxer died, bitten by a venomous snake."

"How can we help you break all these magical spells, and get your lives back to what they were before?" you candidly ask.

"To break all these malevolent spells and free us, there is only one way..." says the queen.

Hurry to section 139

128

"Sir..."

"Not Sir...Captain."

"I'm sorry," you tell the tall soldier. "Captain, please forgive him. He does not realize what he is saying."

"YES I DO!" yells the rude teenager. "WHAT ARE YOU TALKING ABOUT, CHO?!"

At that moment, the captain grabs Raju's arm, unaware of his opponent's impressive abilities. Without any warning, the teenager pulls the muscular man towards him, and executes a fast shoulder throw in the direction of the pyramid! Before he can realize what is happening to him, the captain smashes head first against a stone block, and immediately loses consciousness.

"TAKE THAT, TOUGH GUY!" yells Raju.

The two other soldiers spontaneously turn towards the teen, pulling out their large swords.

"I don't think so..." says Sunita.

She catapults herself towards one of the two soldiers, and smashes her knee into one of the men's face. The poor man doesn't know what hit him, and crumbles to the ground. The last soldier standing lifts his sword and is about to strike Sunita in the back, when he receives one of your fantastic flying kicks across the jaw, sending him down. The young woman smiles at you, then turns to her brother, and screams:

"WHAT IS THE MATTER WITH YOU?! YOU WANT TO GET US KILLED?! LEARN TO SHUT YOUR BIG MOUTH SOMETIMES!!!"

"This big dude started it," answers Raju pointing at the captain. You look at the teenager, and simply say:

"No more of your nonsense, Raju. Listen to your sister. Now let's move on."

You continue walking along the pyramid, searching for a small square opening. You quickly reach the second corner of the pyramid, and turn left. About half way through its length, you stop walking.

"I found something," you tell the twins, "...something we did not expect to find."

"What is it?" asks Sunita.

Both brother and sister stare in disbelief at what you found.

"Great!" says Raju. "There are two identical small square openings! They are cut into the solid rock...side-by-side! How are we supposed to know which one we are looking for?!"

You look inside both openings, and realize you are facing two long tunnels.

"We will have to crawl inside one of these two tunnels. The good thing is that there is a little light coming from the end of both tunnels. This should help us."

If you want to crawl into the right tunnel, good luck in section 124

If you prefer crawling inside the left one, it's time for section 132

129

With great difficulty, you open the iridium door...and step onto a glorious green field filled with multicolored flowers, tall trees, and cute prairie dogs. The stunning sky is crystal clear, and a limpid river flows between two small mountains nearby.

"I'm confused," says Sunita. "What is this place?"

"Who cares!" yaps Raju. "Where's that golden key?"

Instinct. You swiftly grab Sunita and Raju by one arm, and scream:

"LET'S GET OUT OF HERE!!"

But your warning comes too late. The remarkable scenery abruptly changes...and you all find yourselves standing on filthy soil mixed with black burning coal.

"LOOK CHO!" yells Sunita, "WE ARE SURROUNDED BY A DOZEN DRAGONS! THEY ARE BLOWING FIRE INTO THE AIR!!"

At that moment, a deep threatening voice echoes very loudly in the dusty air:

"YOU SHOULD NOT HAVE COME HERE..."

These are the last words you will ever hear. These dragons are unforgiving, and for inexplicable reasons, you are unable to activate any of your magical skills!

THE END

130

"It's unquestionably coming from the back wall," you tell the queen as you hastily walk behind the two majestic thrones. You impulsively press your ear against the wall, and unintentionally push a small stone into the wall! Immediately, a large opening magically appears in the wall...and you unexpectedly see a very frightening gargantuan creature facing you! It is at least eight feet tall, and its massive body, legs, arms, and head are completely covered with long gray hairs. It has no neck, four small piercing eyes, and a wide opened mouth showing nasty teeth.

"THE BEAST!!!" screams Sunita.

With one swift movement of its arm, *The Beast* strikes you, and you fly across the room, crashing into the opposite wall! You hit the hard wall head first...and die instantly. In less than a minute, Queen Killa, King Beltak, and the twins will be joining you permanently in the spirit world. They will try to defend their lives against *The Beast*...but in vain...

So many loved ones will cry for you...

THE END

131

You choose to go right. Following the base of the pyramid, you see that the entire structure is made of large heavy limestone blocks.

"It must have been incredibly challenging to build such an enormous pyramid," you tell Sunita.

"Yes, especially considering the fact that the workers did not have the tools nor the technology we have on Earth today."

"It doesn't impress me," yaps Raju. "A bunch of idiots working with rocks...big deal!"

"So what impresses you?" his sister asks.

"Money and power! Piles of it!!"

A few minutes later, you all reach the pyramid's corner, and turn left. Immediately, you come face-to-face with a Maya sentinel. The group of three armed soldiers asks you right away:

"Who are you and what are you doing here?"

"We are tourists," you simply answer. "We want to visit the pyramid."

"Really?" says the sentinel's captain. "Why didn't you walk up the stairs to reach the main entrance?"

"That's none of your business!" tells him Raju.

"I don't like your tone, young man," continues the muscular captain. "Do you know who you are talking to?"

"Yes...I am talking to an imbecile holding a spear...a dumbbell wearing ugly sandals, thinking he's tough because of the sword hanging from his fancy leather belt."

"RAJU!" screams Sunita. "ENOUGH!"

The captain glares at Raju with his piercing eyes, and says:

"You are going to have to come with me, young insolent."

"Make me," replies Raju.

"That will not be a problem," says the captain.

If you decide to run away, take a chance at section 137

**If you prefer trying to talk with the captain,
be eloquent in section 128. Your life depends on it!**

132

"Let's not waste any more time," you tell the twins. "I vote for the left one!"

You lie down on your stomach, and begin crawling inside the left tunnel. After about five minutes, the tunnel turns into a very wide hallway with a high ceiling, allowing you to stand up.

"Finally!" says Sunita. "We can stretch our bodies!"

"Stop complaining," Raju tells her. "You're a spoiled brat sometimes."

"Oh really?" she replies. "Did you look at yourself in the mirror lately, Mr. I Love To Whine?"

"Come on you two," you tell the immature teenagers.

You continue walking straight towards the light. But after taking about twenty steps, you abruptly stop, staring to your left.

"We found it!" you tell the twins. "We found the bronze door!"

"AMAZING!!" yells Sunita. "WE FINALLY DID IT!"

"GIVE ME THE GOLDEN KEY!" screams Raju. "LET ME SEE WHAT'S BEHIND THIS DOOR!!"

"Hold on," you calmly reply to the young man. "Let me open the door. In your agitated state, I would not want you to break this delicate key."

You slowly take out the red velvet box, and ask Sunita to open it. When she does, you delicately take the golden key out, and insert it inside the door lock. Without making a sound, the door easily opens to a vast room entirely covered with thick square porcelain tiles. You immediately notice that all the tiles are colourfully hand-painted with mysterious Maya symbols.

"This is it," you say.

Raju and Sunita rush past you, into the room...and both start to scream again!

"CHO!! COME QUICKLY!!!"

Hurry to section 123!

133

You decide to walk through the left opening, even though you can't see anything inside. It's complete darkness! There are no torches fixed on the walls, not a single light source, nothing which would allow you to see where you are going.

If you master the skill of owl's eyes, use it in section 138

If you don't, continue walking to section 145

134

To quickly finish you off, the enormous brute throws its huge fist at your face. Swiftly, you move your head out of the way with great agility. At the same time, you abruptly vanish before the monster's eyes! Astonished by your sudden disappearance, *The Beast* turns around and starts searching for you, not realizing you are standing just beside it. In a fantastic spinning back kick, you pulverize the creature's torso in hundreds of pieces. The hideous brute crumbles to the ground, now turned into a pile of steamy rocks.

"I'm glad this is over," you tell yourself.

You dust yourself off, and take one last look at the pile of rocks, to make sure *The Beast* is gone completely.

Run to section 154!

135

King Felipe turns around, and walks back to his royal chair. After comfortably sitting down, he looks at all three of you, and says:

"Since you are here, and I feel that time is of essence for all of you, I will provide you with adequate transportation." He glances in your direction, and continues:

"It is the least that I can do to help in your...'quest'."

"What transportation?" asks Raju. "You want to give us three mules?"

"Raju! Show some respect!!" commands Sunita.

"King Felipe, your help and generosity will not be overlooked," you tell the monarch. "You have my word that this...'quest'...will be successful."

"I have no doubt it will be. I can feel it," says the older man.

He gets up while his gaze sweeps from you to the twins. He lifts up his arms...and says:

"Go and fly across time and mountains! Fulfill your destiny!"

At the same time, a tremendous yellow light resembling an electric current comes out of his hands and eyes before hitting all of you at once! You suddenly find yourself in a gargantuan tunnel of spinning yellow light, flying at an inconceivable speed through many time capsules. You feel as if a harmless blanket of fire was wrapping itself around you, pleasantly heating every part of your body. Your speed increases as you fly through the tunnel, and the spinning yellow light abruptly changes colours every split second!

"WOW! yells Sunita. "THIS IS INCREDIBLE!!!

Swiftly, a celestial white light fills up the tunnel. Its brightness is exquisite but it doesn't hurt your eyes. Slowly, the celestial light disappears, leaving you and the twins standing in front of the Pyramid of the Sun!

Continue your journey at section 122

136

"PREPARE YOURSELF TO JOIN YOUR ANCESTORS!" yells *The Beast*.

It swings its enormous fist at your head but you duck to avoid being hit. Right away, a gigantic rocky foot kicks you like a soccer ball, and sends you rolling onto the floor.

"That was painful," you tell yourself.

"YOU SEE," says the gruesome monster, YOU CAN'T BEAT ME!!"

"Oh really?" you answer with a smile.

Activating the remarkable magic within you, two red laser beams abruptly come out of your eyes! With astonishing power, they crash into the huge creature's head, instantly scorching it!

"NOOOOO! STOOOOOP!" yells *The Beast*.

"Sorry to disappoint you," you coolly reply.

A moment later, the brute's head completely melts along with part of its upper torso. The gargantuan creature falls forward, smashing against the floor.

"That wasn't too bad," you tell yourself.

You dust yourself off, and take one last look at what's left of the pulverized beast.

It's time for section 154...

137

"Follow me!" you whisper to the twins.

You all turn around, and start running in the same direction you came from...

Big mistake...

These men are highly trained soldiers, and they know how to throw a spear. The last thing you will ever feel is an atrocious pain going right through you...before falling face first to the ground.

Sunita and Raju will now join you in your permanent one-way trip to the spirit world...because your mission is over.

THE END

138

During your intense training in Tibet, you learned to see through extreme darkness inside the deepest Himalayan caves, and through the darkest nights. You enabled your eyes to see clearly through the worst obscurity, the same way you can see during a beautiful day. You walk forward, feeling swallowed by this large corridor, as you get deeper and deeper inside it. Abruptly, you stop walking: right in front of you, there is a wide hole in the ground going from one side of the wall to the other. You bend over a little to look inside the hole.

"Something is moving down there," you think to yourself. You take a closer look at what is beneath you, and see water...with crocodiles swimming everywhere...many crocodiles!"

"I'm so glad I can see in the dark! Those crocodiles look very hungry, and I certainly avoided becoming their next meal."

INSTINCT! You turn around...but it's too late! An enormous hairy beast appears out of nowhere behind you, and pushes you into the hole...

In a few seconds, your life will be over. Queen Killa and King Beltak will never be rescued, and the twins will never be stopped. Thanks to you, the world is now doomed forever, and will soon be ruled by the hand of a delusional brother and his sister...

THE END

139

"And what is that way...?" asks Raju in a nonchalant voice.

"*The Beast* must be destroyed," answers the king. "One night, we overheard my brother Wexxer talking to one of his servants about a horrendous creature he had just created. My brother referred to it as *The Beast*. Apparently, it looks like an enormous hairy monster but it is really an artificial life form made of hair and stones. Its strength is beyond words, and it has no mercy. It lives somewhere inside the Pyramid of the Sun, but strangely, we have never seen it. Wexxer bragged to his servant that only *The Beast*'s death could permanently annihilate all the malefic spells cast on our Pyramid.

"But according to Wexxer, *The Beast* is invincible, and therefore all of the spells he cast would last forever," adds the queen.

"Queen Killa...King Beltak...I give you my word that we will find *The Beast*, and annihilate it," you promise the monarchs.

"With all our hearts...thank you!" tells you the grateful queen. "We somehow knew we could count on you."

"Speak for yourself!" suddenly intervenes Raju. "I'm not risking my own life in order to defeat a giant hairy monster!!"

"Nobody is forcing you to help us," retorts the king. "What about you, young lady?"

"I think...that...I will stay with my brother," answers Sunita, a little embarrassed.

"Then I will find this creature by myself," you promptly announce.

BOOM! BOOM! BOOM!

"Again...this same noise..." whispers Sunita.

"It's definitely coming from the back wall," you tell the twins, as you quickly walk towards it. You instinctively press your ear against the wall, and accidentally push a small stone into the wall! Instantaneously, two large openings magically appear side-by-side in the massive stone wall! Both openings are dark and uninviting but easily accessible. You turn around to look at the twins, and say:

"Last chance to come with me..."

"No way!" barks Raju as Sunita simply looks down. You wave to the monarchs as the queen says:

"Come back to us alive!"

"I will," you answer. You turn around, and look ahead...

"Each opening looks like some kind of dark hallway," you think to yourself. *"Where should I go?"*

If you choose to walk through the left opening,
prepare yourself for section 133

If you prefer going through the right opening,
walk to section 143

140

"YOU THINK YOU CAN DEFEAT ME?!" screams *The Beast*.

It violently pushes you, sending you flying against one of the walls. You spring back to your feet, opening a huge flow of magic from inside you. Quickly, you extend your arms in front, and open both of your hands wide. A split second later, fire jets come out of your hands, and hit the monster's colossal legs. *The Beast* is forced to take a few steps back, and starts laughing:

"HA! HA! HA! YOU'RE GOING TO HAVE TO DO BETTER THAN THAT TO STOP ME!"

"As you wish," you answer.

Another powerful set of fire jets immediately come out of your hands...and this time out of your eyes too!!! The inferno crashes straight into *The Beast*, as you send a continuous flow of burning fire jets. The repulsive monster heats up to the point that it suddenly explodes, turning into a pile of burning coal!

"Who is laughing now?" you say out loud.

You feel proud as you stare one last time at the burning flames, and at the pile of what used to be *THE BEAST.*

Continue your journey at section 154

141

"I SHALL ELEMINATE YOU!" screams *The Beast.*

"Good luck with that," you tell the dreadful monster.

Without prior notice, it blows out air so hard at you that it propels you back a few feet away to the dusty floor.

"HA! HA! HA! HA!" laughs the gigantic creature. "I BET YOU WERE NOT EXPECTING THAT!"

In response, you throw a massive iron bolt at the monster's abdomen, instantly pulverizing it with amazing force. *The Beast* transforms itself into a stack of rocks before falling to the grimy floor.

"I bet you were not expecting THAT!" you think to yourself.

You dust yourself off, and take one last look at what used to be *The Beast.*

Take a deep breath before reaching section 154...

142

You and the twins appear in the middle of a vast unfinished ballroom where there is a very strong moldy smell. The floor, the walls, and ceiling are partially covered with plywood sheets, and you see many contractors around you. They are working hard to finish building the room. Raju smirks at them, and says:

"How pathetic! This room was supposed to be finished a long time ago, and these lazy workers are still not done. What a bunch of incompetents!"

"Relax brother," says Sunita. "None of this is of importance anymore."

"What do you mean?" asks the young man.

"Cho," continues the young lady, "may I please borrow your crown?"

**If you agree to lend your golden crown to Sunita,
give it to her in section 147**

If you prefer not to, continue to section 151

143

"I have a good feeling about the opening on the right," you tell yourself. *"Let's go!"*

You step inside but you can't see where you are going. You let your hand slide against the wall, to feel the path you are taking.

"I hate this obscurity!" you tell yourself. Out of nowhere, just as this thought crosses your mind, a red light magically illuminates the part of the stone hallway where you are. Immediately, you stop breathing! About twenty feet away from you, you see a massive silhouette walking your away. As it gets closer, you suddenly realize what it is...

...It is at least eight feet tall, and its immense head, body, arms, and legs are completely covered with thick long gray hair. It has no neck, small piercing eyes, and a wide opened mouth showing terrible teeth.

"The Beast..." you whisper.

"I AM SURPRISED YOU FOUND THE GOLDEN KEY," says *The Beast* with a terribly daunting voice. "YOU ARE MORE CLEVER THAN I THOUGHT. WELL IT DOES NOT MATTER NOW...BECAUSE YOU WILL DIE."

If you master the skill of invisibility, disappear in section 134

If you are a fire jet master, use your skill at section 140

If you master the art of laser eyes, heat up your eyes at section 136

If you possess the skill of iron bolt,
now would be a great time to use it in section 141

If you wish to use your ice bolt skill, start cooling your hands in section 150

If you are a telekinesis master, get ready for section 144

If you choose to fight *The Beast* using only your martial arts expertise,
good luck in section 148!

144

"THIS IS THE END OF YOU!" yells *The Beast.*

"We shall see..." you answer while activating your telekinetic ability.

"YOU ARE RIGHT! I SHALL SEE YOU IN PIECES!"

To your great surprise, the horrific monster throws a powerful series of deadly kicks and punches at you. You deflect every deadly blow, but you accidently trip backwards due to an irregularity in the floor. The horrendous creature immediately jumps into the air in an attempt to crush you with its massive weight...but it is stopped in mid-air! It floats above the ground, now wiggling like a puppet, as you deeply stare at it.

"WHAT'S GOING ON?!" yells *The Beast.*

You get back onto your feet, and say:

"It's called telekinesis. I am the one controlling what is happening to you...with my mind."

"PUT ME DOWN NOW!" orders the hideous monster.

"With pleasure."

With unbelievable force, you smash *The Beast* onto the floor so fiercely that it shatters into pieces! Immediately, you feel that something is changing in the air, as if a strange metamorphosis was suddenly happening all around you...

You take one last look at *The Beast* to make sure that it is eliminated.

Hurry to section 154!

145

"I can't see where I'm going! I guess as I walk, I will let my hand slide on one of the walls in order to feel where this corridor takes me."

You do not have to go far to discover something hazardous...like a wide treacherous hole, in the rocky ground, going from one wall to the other, which you could not see in this obscurity.

"NOOOOO!" you scream as you fall down. A few seconds later, you hit a large body of icy water.

"IT'S SO COLD!"

Something hard and very rough unexpectedly touches your hand: a very long, thick and scaly tail!

"A CROCODILE! OH NO!!!!!"

These are the last words you will ever say...

Now all the people in our world and far beyond will forever suffer because of you. You drastically failed your mission, and let everybody down. Why did you have to keep walking forward if you could not see where you were going?

THE END

146

"Cho, you have freed the Pyramid of the Sun, and all our people from an appalling curse. Thanks to you, *The Beast* has been defeated. As of now, we can all go on living normal lives."

"We will be eternally grateful to you for your incommensurable help," continues King Beltak. "As a sign of our gratitude to you, please accept my golden crown. It will grant you two wishes every day, for the rest of your life..."

"King Beltak," you answer uneasily, "I couldn't possibly accept your gift.

It is YOUR crown, and you are the only one who deserves to wear it."

"But Cho, you gave us our lives back. If someone truly deserves to have it, it is you. You must accept it."

"Remember," adds the queen, "magical wishes must not hurt people in any way. I know your heart is pure, but if someone other than you would put on this crown, and wish for something unfavorable and damaging, the crown would disappear forever..."

"I will remember your words. Queen Killa and King Beltak: thank you," you tell the monarchs.

"We are the ones who are thanking you," says the king as he puts his crown on your head. "You are free to stay here as long as you like."

"I appreciate your invitation, King Beltak. Forgive me, but I must leave at once to fulfill...a duty."

"We understand," replies Queen Killa. "Our door will always be open should you ever come back."

You bow to the queen and king before rejoining Sunita. She greets you with a smile and says:

"Congratulations Cho in defeating *The Beast*! Somehow I knew you could do it."

"I'm glad it's over," you simply answer.

"I'm sorry," she continues, "but I was a little scared to follow you, down that dark hallway, to face a giant scary monster."

"I wasn't scared!" says Raju who joins the conversation.

"Don't worry about it," you tell the sister. "It's normal to feel scared sometimes. The important thing is to learn to control your fear, so it doesn't control you."

"What?" asks Raju in a rude tone.

"Listen Cho," says Sunita, "I will never forget that you saved my brother's life...and you did it in such a startling way!"

"I'm happy it all ended well...and that Raju is alive."

"I would like to invite you back to our palace in Kathmandu," continues the young lady. "It's the least we could do to properly thank you, right Raju?"

"I guess," mumbles the loathsome teenager, "but it's not finished yet. I'm sure there is still a lot of work to be done."

"That's alright," you reply. "I'm sure it will be grandiose, and I won't be staying too long anyway."

"At least a few days," says Sunita.

"Going to their palace gives me another opportunity to bring them to Gutuk, the gate keeper of time," you tell yourself. *"I must wait for the right moment to neutralize them, in order to take them with me to see Gutuk, in the akashic records..."*

Sunita takes her brother's hand after taking yours, closes her eyes, and whispers:

"We are now all leaving this time capsule...to go back to Earth...to our palace in Kathmandu."

You close your eyes, and immediately feel your body's molecules starting to vibrate quickly. You feel as your body is lifted up higher and higher by a gentle force. Before you know it, you are back in the tunnel of marvelous white light, flying at an astonishing speed...

"This feeling is truly out of this world," you tell yourself.

A short moment later, you open your eyes...

Fly to section 142...

147

Realizing what is about to happen, you agree to hand the golden head piece to Sunita as she smiles at you. She puts the crown on her head, and says:

"I wish for this palace to be entirely completed as follows: all the floors, walls, and ceilings must be made with solid gold, and our architectural plans must be respected carefully throughout the palace. I want to see a perfect balance of diamonds, other precious stones, and pure silver to be used for all faucets, handles, and doorknobs. All windows must be made out of the clearest crystal, and I want the heat to be perfectly adjusted at all time. I also want to see exotic plants, rare paintings, and twenty four carat gold sculptures to be placed throughout, with style..."

All around you, the air suddenly becomes very bubbly. You are quickly surrounded by thick bubbles of clouds which are so dense that you can't see anything else!

"Wow!" you tell yourself. *"It's as if I was just submerged inside a giant glass of sparking water."*

Gracefully, the bubbles start to disappear, and you can't believe what you are seeing! Your eyes are now seeing a completely finished palace, exactly the way Sunita wished it to be. Remarkable rare paintings from all over the world are hanging from the golden walls. Various gold sculptures and other artifacts are placed throughout the room, along with gorgeous exotic plants. Priceless diamond chandeliers are hanging from the gilded ceiling, illuminating the marvelous room in a spectacular way! Through the many lavish crystal windows, the midnight blue coloured night swiftly took over the sky, and wrapped itself around the snow covered Himalayan mountains.

"And this is how it's done!!" proudly states Sunita.

"Impressive," you say out of politeness.

"WAY TO GO!" screams Raju. "What a brilliant idea you had! I'm surprised I didn't think of it."

He launches forward at his sister, and brusquely yanks the magical crown off her head, before putting it on his own.

"HEY!" snaps the young woman at her brother. He quickly says out loud:

"I wish for this palace to be permanently filled with all the food, drinks, servants, gold bullions and all other luxuries I want!"

Within a few seconds, an incredibly bright light fills up the majestic room, to the point where you have to shut your eyes from the intense luster. A moment later, the radiant light disappears, and you open your eyes. Once again, you are in awe. In front of you, you see six massive silvery tables filled with various hot and cold fancy dishes, luscious drinks and delectable pastries. Each large silvery table is set to serve sixteen people, and is surrounded by sixteen solid gold chairs. Elegantly placed in each corner of the room, you notice very large stacks of gold bullions almost reaching the ceiling.

"THAT'S HOW IT'S DONE SISTER!" yells the pretentious and greedy young man. "NOW LET'S ALL ENJOY THIS FEAST!!"

Swiftly, servants fill up three blue porcelain plates with scrumptious Nepalese delicacies. Along with the twins, you sit down at one of the colossal ornate tables, and are immediately served a tall glass of fresh marmelo juice. You take a sip, and ask Sunita:

"What's in this juice? It's truly delicious! It has a litchi taste to it."

"Yes it does," answers the young lady, "but it is a whole lot healthier. The marmelo fruit, also called bel, resembles red currents, and is filled with vitamins and minerals. The use of marmelos in Nepal is well known as a cardio tonic, to treat indigestion, and to improve memory. Bel juice also gives you great energy and fights chronic fatigue."

"I hate it," says Raju as three elegantly dressed-men put a mouth-watering plate of hot steamy food in front of each of you. "You are such a walking encyclopedia!"

"I recognize these savory dumplings," you say. "They are called momos. I had them in Kathmandu."

"Good for you," yaps Raju with his mouth full.

"RAJU!" reacts Sunita. "You are talking to the person who saved your life. Have some respect! If it wasn't for Cho, we would not have this food to eat or any of this!"

In an awkward silence, the three servants quietly step away as you start tasting the delightful steamy food in front of you.

Continue to fill up your hungry tummy at section 149

148

"YOU DON'T STAND A CHANCE AGAINST ME!" yells *The Beast.* It slowly walks up to you, and says while punching its hairy abdomen:

"COME ON! GIVE ME YOUR BEST SHOT!"

"If you insist," you answer plainly.

With incredible power, you jump towards the creature, and deliver an extraordinary blow to its solar plexus with your fist. In a fantastic explosion, the monster instantaneously turns into a pile of stones, pulverized by your startling hit.

"A reign of terror has ended," you tell yourself.

You straighten yourself up, and observe the pile that was left behind, after your surprisingly short encounter with *The Beast.*

It's time to go to section 154

149

After eating one of the most delicious meals you've ever had in your life, Raju abruptly stands up, and announces:

"I have to admit that this meal was very tasty. It's a good thing we have this magical crown."

"You mean a crown that belongs to Cho," says Sunita.

Ignoring his sister's comment, the young pretentious man continues:

"I don't know about you two, but I'm very tired, so I'm going to bed. Cho, make yourself at home."

He leaves you and Sunita sitting at the table. She looks at you and starts talking:

"Do you realize the power of this magical crown? Cho, we could all be the wealthiest people on the planet! We could buy everything and everyone! We could even rule the world!!"

"Are those the values your parents taught you?" you ask the young lady. "To become the richest person on Earth and to lead the world? To what end?"

"Power," says a familiar voice behind you. You turn around and see Raju standing nearby. He walks up to you and says:

"This magical crown is the answer to all of our problems and worries. Since it grants two wishes per day to the person who is wearing it, imagine the long term benefits and possibilities: absolutely endless!"

You take a look at the golden crown that was left on the table by your plate. You then realize what a dangerous weapon it could become if it would fall into the wrong set of hands.

"Cho, don't you want to be filthy rich?" asks Sunita.

"It depends...I want to be rich differently than you do: I want to help people," you simply answer. "There is more to life than focusing on becoming the financially wealthiest person on the planet."

"Life gave us the unique opportunity to become wealthy beyond our wildest dreams!" continues Raju. "Cho, you want to help people? You will need money for that...lots of it! By the same token, we can all share the benefits of having never-ending wealth."

"We didn't ask for this crown," ads the young woman. "It was offered to you as a gift. Since you have the crown in our palace, it would be silly for all of us not to take advantage of it."

"I agree," says a young woman behind Raju.

Instinct!

Hurry to section 165...quickly!!!

150

"I WILL CRUSH YOU LIKE A BUG!" says the gruesome monster.

"I don't think so," you calmly reply.

Demonstrating an unexpected agility and great flexibility, *The Beast* suddenly lifts up its gigantic leg very high. It executes a perfect standing up split in order to throw a deadly hammer kick at your head, but you know better. Out of the blue, you throw three massive ice bolts at the atrocious monster, completely freezing it upon impact!

"You are not so tough now, are you?" you tell *The Beast*.

You calmly walk to the hideous creature, and send it to the ground with the push of one hand. The creature's very heavy body smashes onto the stone floor, and shatters under the powerful impact.

Section 154 is now waiting for you...

151

"I am sorry Sunita, but I prefer not to," you tell the teenager.

"Why?" asks the young lady.

Without answering, you simply step back while looking at her staggered expression. Out of the blue, the weak floor unexpectedly collapses where you are standing! You have nowhere to go but down...about thirty feet below...

Your body crashes against the hard cement floor, and the violent impact instantaneously takes your life away. You were so close to completing your mission...but you drastically failed. Accidents can obviously be very costly.

Unfortunately, the twins will take the golden crown from you, and become the ultimate rulers of the world! So many people and families are now doomed to suffer...endlessly.

THE END

152

Prem launches at you with his kukra knife, but he does not realize who he is up against. You sweep the hand holding the knife before applying a strong pressure against his wrist. Immediately, Prem drops his weapon, as his body is flipped through the air. He crashes with force against Kishor who was also charging at you. With two men down so quickly, Raju throws himself at Bibek, yelling:

"ARE YOU READY FOR ME, PUNK?"

Both of them throw dangerous blows at each other but manage to either block or duck.

"You're going down!" says Raju.

"You're so annoying," answers Bibek as he tries to land a reverse roundhouse kick.

You run to Sunita to give her a hand against the twin sisters. After swiftly kicking off their fancy shoes, both Heena and Pragya attack Sunita with a series of low and high kicks. So far, Sunita manages to fight them off brilliantly, using impressive techniques. Suddenly, Sunita jumps in the air, and lands a beautiful back spinning kick across Heena's cheek.

"One down and one to go," says Sunita looking at the now unconscious Heena.

"She doesn't need my help," you say to yourself.

Unexpectedly, a powerful right uppercut sends Sunita to the floor. Pragya approaches her blacked out opponent, and says:

"Who is down now?"

You sneak up to her before replying:

"Actually, you are."

With a single finger, you swiftly apply a strong pressure on her upper spine. She is quickly out cold...and now lying next to her sister.

You then glance at the action between Raju and Bibek..

Get to section 162... fast!

153

Elegantly, the twin sisters take their expensive red shoes off. They look at you, Sunita, and Raju before saying:

"The gold crown is now ours!"

"Not even in your dreams," answers Sunita.

"It's time to heat things up…" you tell yourself as you open a large flow of magic inside of you. You can now feel the fire coming to the surface of your hands. Without any warning, you throw five quick fire jets at your opponents, aiming for their weapons. The fire hits the knives with great force, slightly burning their hands.

"Aaaaaaahhhhh!" scream the assailants, as they drop their kukra knives.

"CHO!" yells Raju. "HOW DID YOU DO THAT?!"

"Cho…" says Sunita.

"This is crazy!" says Prem. "I'm not fighting a fakir shooting fire out of his hands!"

"We're with you!" add Kishor and Heena.

With great fear in their eyes, they look at you one last time before running away.

"COWARDS!" screams Raju as he throws a series of punches and kicks at Bibek who manages to duck every blow.

"I WANT THAT CROWN!!" yells Pragya as she throws a reverse roundhouse kick to Sunita's face. Still deeply shocked by your magic display, Sunita does not react fast enough, and gets kicked on the side of her head. She instantly falls down unconscious. At once, you propel yourself towards Pragya before striking her with your thumb on the side of her neck. By doing so, your calculated pressure knocks her out instantaneously.

It's time to help Raju in section 162!

154

"This pyramid is now forever free of all spells," you say out loud.

You start walking back towards the room where you left the twins. As you walk, you notice that everything is changing around you: the grimy stone floor starts to shine and sparkle in an odd way, before metamorphosing itself into stunning green marble plates! The same phenomenon swiftly happens to the walls, ceiling, and light fixtures which suddenly appear out of thin air!

"The spells are truly broken, and everything is changing back to how it used to be," you think to yourself. *"What a relief!"*

You quickly reach the end of the hallway before stepping into the room, where books were flying in a large circular motion. Stunned by what you are seeing, you stand still…

Throughout the large rectangular room, you notice at least eight beautifully carved wooden tables on which a variety of delightful food has been placed. On one side of the room, seven brilliant musicians, with flutes and drums, are playing joyful music while laughing together. Dozens of well-dressed women and men are standing around the tables, celebrating. They are eating together, dancing, hugging each other, happy to be alive and free of the terrible spells cast on the pyramid. You are deeply impressed by the dazzling long dresses the women are wearing, and the chic suits worn by the men. You also notice that the entire room's floor and walls are now covered with beautiful limestone tiles, plaster masks, and other jeweled artifacts.

"This is amazing..." you think to yourself.

Marvelous paintings are hanging on the walls, depicting the history of the Pyramid of the Sun and its people. Strategically placed, large exotic plants are delicately adding a touch of grace to the rich decor while delightfully perfuming the air. On top of all of these wonders, you notice spectacular large windows in the wall behind you, through which the majestic blue sky is safely wrapping the world. In one corner of the room, you see Raju stuffing his mouth with delicate desserts while Sunita is pleasantly conversing with people around her. Swiftly, the music stops playing. Every woman and man in the room slowly turns your way...

"Am I so badly dressed that people are staring at me?" you think to yourself half-jokingly.

Holding one another's hand, elevated between their shoulders as if they were gracefully dancing, Queen Killa and King Beltak unhurriedly walk up to you with a large smile on their faces. They both bow to you before being imitated by their guests. The queen then speaks:

Prepare yourself for section 146...

155

Without waiting a second, you begin spinning in place at a tremendous speed. You then open your arms to further expand what you are about to become...You are now spinning so fast that you are suddenly invisible, creating all around your body an extremely powerful sandy whirlwind...finally turning yourself into a tornado!

"NO WAY!" yells Raju.

"This can't be," mumbles Sunita.

You slide on the floor towards your five attackers who now have a petrified look in their eyes.

"A FAKIR FROM HELL!" screams Prem. "LET'S GET OUT OF HERE!"

"NO!" orders Pragya. "I WANT THAT CROWN!!"

As Heena, Prem and Kishor run away, Pragya tackles Sunita to the ground. Raju' sister hits her head against the solid gold floor, and passes out. But a second later, the long funnel-shaped cloud you have become touches Pragya, and catapults her against Bibek. She is out cold, unconscious, but he manages to get up...

Prepare yourself for section 146...

156

You take a deep breath to feel the energy all around the room. You feel this marvelous force penetrating every molecule of your body, filling it up completely. You then direct all this energy around your forearm while executing a large circular movement with your arm. An instant later, you are holding the impenetrable heavenly shield.

"I can't believe my eyes," says Sunita staring at you holding your shield.

"WOW!" yells Raju. "AND YOU DID NOT TELL US YOU WERE A FAKIR THIS WHOLE TIME?"

Instinct. You jump in front of Sunita and Raju before sweeping the air with your shield. You immediately hear a metallic noise and see five kukra knives at your feet.

"Ha!" says Raju. "Throwing your knives at us was a really brainless move on your part! Now you will make our job way easier."

You jumps towards Prem and Kishor before hitting them in the abdomen with your shield. Feeling great pain, the two men fall to the ground, trying to catch a breath. Raju immediately throws himself at Bibek to neutralize him as fast as possible, while Sunita pushes Pragya against Heena. They both end up on the ground.

"It's not that easy fighting in high-heels, is it?" smirks Sunita.

The twin sisters swiftly take off their fancy shoes, and launch at Sunita. Once again, you come to her rescue, this time by strongly pushing away Heena with your shield. She picks up two kukra knives from the floor to attack you, but she is no match for you. You hit her hands with your shield to make her drop the knives, before striking her with a finger on the side of her head. She passes out instantly. You turn around and see Pragya observing you...next to an unconscious Sunita lying on the floor.

"She's just taking a nap," arrogantly says Pragya.

"You should too," you tell the young lady as you propel yourself at her, before applying a pressure with your thumb to the base of her neck. She passes out in your arms before you lay her on the floor. You quickly glance at Raju as he is being abruptly pushed back by Bibek...

Prepare yourself for section 162!

157

Slowly, like a pair of lionesses hunting for their prey, Pragya and Heena take off their high-heel shoes, and dash towards Sunita. Unexpectedly, she jumps towards the twin sisters, and throws a powerful back spinning kick. She smashes her heel into Heena's face before sending her to the ground, knocking her out completely.

"Nice kick sister!" says Raju.

"There is more where that came from," answers Sunita.

"You think you can stop us?" says Kishor.

"We can try," you answer the 'knife expert'. You open a flow of magic inside of you, and start accelerating the vibration of your body's molecules. To your audience's disbelief, your body starts to become transparent... before completely disappearing!

"UNREAL!" says Raju.

"A real fakir..." mumbles Sunita, taking her attention away from her opponent for a moment. All of a sudden, she receives a solid right hook across the jaw that sends her straight to the ground.

"Ha! Ha! You won't be getting up so soon!" laughs Pragya. But she is unable to see you running up to her...

"Sweet dreams," you whisper in her ear as you apply a special pressure with your index finger to her solar plexus. Comatose, the she falls in your arms before you lay her down on the floor. You immediately run to Prem and Kishor, and put them asleep the same away.

"YOU GUYS ARE DROPPING LIKE FLIES!" yells Raju as he attacks Bibek with various roundhouse kicks.

"But you are next," answers his opponent.

It's time for section 162!

158

You open a wonderful flow of magic living inside you, and feel your hands becoming colder and colder. Unexpectedly, you swiftly throw five massive ice bolts at your opponents. Almost all your ice bolts reach their targets...except one! In front of you, the twin sisters, Prem and Kishor now look like impressive sculptures carved in the thickest ice, but Bibek is lying on his stomach, staring at you.

"I have heard of all sorts of fakirs," he says, "but I have never heard of anybody with your skills!"

Sunita and Raju simply stare at you in disbelief, totally speechless. Bibek quickly sees the opportunity to retaliate, and launches at a startled Sunita. He brusquely tackles her before she hits her head against one of the solid gold chairs. He springs back to his feet, leaving her unconscious on the ground...

Watch out for section 162!

159

Followed by her twin sister Heena, Pragya kicks off her high-heel shoes, and starts running towards Raju' sister.

"You will regret this," thinks Sunita.

She grabs an empty water jug from the table behind her, and throws it at Pragya. The jug crashes against the woman's forehead before sending her to the ground, now completely knocked out.

"Take that!" says Sunita, as she immediately rolls onto the ground in order to avoid Heena's attack, who was just behind her sister.

"You will pay for what you have done to Pragya," says Heena as she extends her arm holding the knife in front of her. Out of nowhere, a red laser beam hits her hand, and makes her drop her weapon.

"Aaaaahhhhhh!" she screams in pain.

"WHAT IN THE WORLD WAS THAT?!" yells Raju as he looks at you. "RED BEAMS JUST CAME OUT OF YOUR EYES!! HOW....?"

"No time to explain," you quickly answer.

Raju runs and throws a flying kick at Bibek while his accomplices, Prem and Kishor, launch at you with their knives. Once again, red laser beams come out of your eyes, and crash against the weapons held by your attackers.

"Aaaaaaahhhhh!" they both yell as they drop their knives.

You instantaneously jump high in front of them, extending both of your legs forward before kicking each man directly in the face.

"These guys won't get up for a while," you tell yourself.

To your left, you see Sunita and Heena exchanging a series of powerful punches and kicks. Suddenly, Heena manages to tackle her opponent as they fall together towards a table. Before hitting the ground, Sunita's head hits the edge of the table with great force, knocking her out.

"SUNITA!" screams Raju as he continues to fight with Bibek.

As Heena grabs back her knife, you dash towards her. Before she can use her weapon, you reach her and strike the central nerve point at the back of her head with two fingers. The young woman collapses to the ground, now unconscious.

Hurry to section 162!

160

"The outside light going into the cave should help me see," you tell yourself.

You step inside and, helped by the daylight coming in, you are able to see the impressive size of this cave. Giant pointy stalactites are hanging from the ceiling, and the walls are covered with grey boulders. Once again, you unexpectedly hear the same sound as before.

"I don't know what it is with this sound, but there is something very pleasant about it that really intrigues me. It's as if a powerful magnet was pulling me..."

You keep walking forward, hoping to quickly discover the origin of the sound. But the deeper you go inside the cave, the less you can see...until it is complete darkness around you.

"Great! Now how can I move forward?" you say out loud.

All of a sudden, the entire cave starts to shake. You can hear big rocks s detaching from the walls, and rolling down towards you.

"An earthquake! What do I do?"

If you choose to run to the right wall,
don't waste any time to reach section 172

If you prefer running towards the left wall,
do it at section 167

161

You take your hands off of the twins' heads, and gently press on their shoulders, and say:

"Don't worry. Everything is fine. Stay seated. It's almost over."

"WHAT?"

Raju springs back to his feet followed by Sunita.

"What is over?" asks Sunita. "Cho? What happened? What's going on?"

"I'll tell you what's going on: Cho is some kind of weird fakir with special powers, who made the gold crown disappear in order for us not to have it!"

Raju turns around and sees Gutuk floating behind him.

"YOU AGAIN?" yaps Raju. "WHAT DO YOU WANT OLD MAN?"

Sunita looks at you softly, visibly confused and now in panic mode. She asks you in a trembling voice:

"Cho..is it true? Did you make the gold crown disappear?"

At that moment, Gutuk touches the twins' heads, trying to finish what he had started. Raju quickly moves away, and says:

"Sunita! Something's not right. Let's meet at our secret hideout! Cho, you will never see us again!"

"WAIT!" you yell...

...but it's too late.

Just like that, the twins have now disappeared out of your site...forever...through the corridors of time. You have greatly disappointed Gutuk who must now accept the aftermath of the twins' bad choices. He will remain the gate keeper of time, and will never see the twins again...

...and you have failed your mission. You were closer than ever! What a shame.

THE END

162

All of a sudden, Bibek starts to run towards the table, where you were previously eating.

"HE'S GOING FOR THE CROWN!" screams Raju. "CHO! STOP HIM!!"

Bibek literally throws himself forward, across the table, before landing on his stomach. He grabs the crown, puts it on his head and says:

"Step back...or else..."

"Give me the crown back," orders Raju, "and I promise you that you will still be in one piece when you leave my palace!"

"You know," says proudly Bibek, "what you both don't realize, is that it's already after midnight. This means that I can make two wishes immediately because it's officially a new day!"

"DON'T YOU DARE DO IT!" yells Raju.

"Actually...do it," you tell Bibek. Both he and Raju look at you as if you just fell from the moon. "You want to become the ultimate ruler of the world? You want to be the richest and most powerful man on Earth? Think about it...this is your chance. I personally don't care about the crown. You want it? It's yours."

"CHO?! WHAT IS THE MATTER WITH YOU??!" screams Raju.

"Think about it," you calmly repeat. "You could now be the most powerful man on the planet...and filthy rich too! Everyone could be your servant. You could have anything you want..."

"QUIET CHO!!!"

You see Bibek's eyes becoming more and more excited after each word you say. His trembling hands rapidly grab the crown on his head. You see his forehead slowly get covered with sweat as his imagination runs wild. Finally, he yells in excitement:

"I WANT TO BE THE MOST POWERFUL MAN ON EARTH...THE RICHEST...THE MOST FEARED! I WANT EVERYONE TO OBEY ME AND TO BE AT MY FEET!"

"Excellent," you tell Bibek.

A second later, the crown slowly disappears from Bibek's head... forever...

"HEY! WHAT'S GOING ON?" he says in a panicked voice. "WHERE'S THE CROWN?"

"NOOOOOOOOOOOOO!!!!" screams Raju at the top of his lungs, understanding what just happened.

Fuming with anger, he runs up to a shocked Bibek, and knocks him out with a very powerful right hook. Raju rapidly turns around and stares at you, outraged:

"You did this on purpose," he says in an almost imperceptible voice. "You wanted the crown to disappear so we would not have it. Who are you really, Cho?"

You just glance at him, not answering.

"I don't really care who you are and what abilities you have! I don't care if you saved my life. What I know...is that you will have to pay for ruining my life...and my sister's!"

"Don't do anything foolish," you tell the pretentious teenager.

"No...that was your job," he replies.

He immediately attacks you with a series of vicious kicks, and strikes. You simply move back or sideways, letting his dangerous blows hit nothing more than the air. You see the terrible anger in his eyes, and the great frustration on his face.

"WHY CHO? WHY?"

He then throws a direct jab at your face. You deflect his punch, and easily throw him against one of the tables. He falls to the ground before springing back to his feet, ready to continue.

"A real martial artist is able to control himself," you tell Raju. "You can't touch me because you are overwhelmed with anger."

"YOU DON'T KNOW ANYTHING!"

He manages to grab one of your arms, but you flip him onto the ground using a classic Tibetan wrist throw. Right away, with your index, you apply a pressure behind one of his ears. Immediately, Raju passes out, now completely comatose. You look at the teenager lying on the floor, feeling pity for him.

"I'm sorry Raju, but I had no other choice."

Your journey continues at section 168

163

As if you had foreseen the terrible danger, three huge stalactites break away from the ceiling and fall straight at you! You jump to your right, and start running to find some kind of shelter from the falling rocks and stalactites...

Regrettably, you trip over a medium-size rock, and land head first into a large boulder. The shock to your head is violent, and leaves you no chance of survival. Maybe stepping inside this cave was not such a good idea...

THE END

164

Your special training in Tibet taught you how to breathe under water forever! You learned to take the water in your mouth, extract the air from it, and fill up your lungs with oxygen, before releasing the water and taking more fresh water in.

You quickly go under water as you feel a steel projectile fly just above your head! As fast as you can, you swim deeper and deeper to get away from the surface. Nonetheless, you see a few more harpoons brutally pierce the water right by you.

"Why are these women trying to eliminate me?" you ask yourself while continuing to swim and breathe under water.

After breathing under water for about ten minutes, a very large sphere of golden light appears not too far from you! It illuminates everything around you. Intrigued by it, you swim towards the sphere, observing it closely. You then stop a few inches from it, wondering what exactly you are looking at. Instinctively, you reach out with your hand, and touch the warm golden sphere.

"Extraordinary!" you tell yourself. *"This sphere feels like warm gelatin..."*

At that moment, you hear the same odd but pleasant sound you heard before entering the cave...as you are propelled inside the sphere!

Get ready for section 166!

165

You swiftly get off your chair, and look behind Raju as Sunita does the same. A young woman dressed in an elegant white blouse and black dressy pants is staring straight at Sunita. She has long black hair, dark eyes, and is wearing sleek red high-heeled shoes. To her left stands another young woman who looks exactly like her! To her right, three wide-shouldered men, dressed in chic white shirts, black slick trousers, and dark snazzy shoes, are staring at you and Raju.

"My name is Pragya and this is my twin sister Heena," says the woman with the red heels.

"So what? Guess who I am?" replies sarcastically Raju.

"I recognize all of you from before," you tell Pragya. "You were part of the group serving the delightful food and drinks."

"Indeed," responds one of the three men. "My name is Bibek. While cleaning up the tables with my friends Prem, Kishor and the twin sisters, I heard what was said about some magical golden crown..."

"This does not concern you," cuts in Raju. "It was a private conversation for our ears only, not yours...so you're all fired! Get out of my palace!"

"I don't think so," replies Heena.

Prem, one of the three men, slowly walks up to one of the tables still covered with appetizing food. He takes a skewer with filet mignon...and starts eating it while looking at Raju who immediately reacts:

"Leave this food, you servant! It's not for you!"

Prem answers in a very calm voice: "This is the way it's going to happen: we will all share the benefits of the magical golden crown..."

"During the next month," continues Bibek, "we will all meet here every morning at 9:00am for a sumptuous breakfast. At that time, one of my friends will wear the crown and make one wish. Then, someone from your group will make the second wish while wearing the headpiece."

"This way," adds Kishor, "it's fair, and we all share the benefits of this magical crown."

"Why should we agree to your demands?" asks Sunita.

"If you don't, we will simply take the crown away from you by force," states Prem.

"I'm trembling!" yaps Raju.

"Trust me, you don't want to mess with us," says Heena. "We are all expert fighters with the kukra knife..."

In one swift movement, all five crooks pull out a knife with an inwardly curved blade, resembling a curved machete.

"You think you can impress us with your toys?" barks Raju. He rolls up his sleeves as he says: "You want the crown? So come and get it!"

"With pleasure," responds Pragya.

If you are a laser eyes master, get ready for section 159

If you are able to become invisible, disappear in section 157

If you have the fire jet skill, heat things up in section 153!

**If you are able to transform yourself into a tornado,
sweep the air at section 155**

If you master the magical skill of ice bolt, run to section 158

**If you want to use your heavenly shield,
now would be a good time in section 156**

**If you don't have the above skills or prefer not to use any,
defend your life in section 152**

166

You fly at an inconceivable speed through a vast tunnel of shiny silver light! You have the impression of being propelled, by a dominant invisible force, through space and amongst billions of stars! You close your eyes and let yourself be caressed by a gentle wind sliding on your face and through your hair. Everything around you then becomes white, as you feel your speed slowing down...before you finally end up sitting!

You open your eyes and realize that you are on a wooden floor, in the middle of a small rustic room. The walls and ceiling are built with thick cedar logs pleasantly perfuming the air. Right in front of you, you see a beautiful red brick fireplace in which a large pot is hanging over a small wood burning fire. Next to the fire, an older man is looking at you while mixing a delicious meal, now boiling inside the pot. He is humming a delicate melody...the sound you have heard before stepping into the cave! He is wearing sandals, and some kind of brown tunic with a rope tied around his waist.

"Would you like some meat stew, *Chosen One*?" asks the man.

"No thank you."

"You don't know what you're missing. It's my specialty."

"Forgive me. How do you know who I am?"

"I am Pelmut, a good friend of Gutuk."

"I see. Where am I?"

"You are inside my golden sphere, in another dimension of the akashic records. You are free to leave when you want simply by visualizing where you want to go."

"Why am I here, Pelmut?"

"I wanted to talk to you, *Chosen One,* so I started to hum a pleasant melody. When you were near the cave, you didn't really know what the pleasant sound was, but it lured you in. Then, upon entering the cave, my magic touch brought you to me."

"You have magical skills?" you ask with enthusiasm.

"Very few," answers Pelmut. "I can make people come to me...and I can see images of the future."

"Fascinating! May I ask you who are all these women, inside that cave, dressed in diving suits, who threw me in a huge pool of hot water?"

"These are my...guardians. They make sure nobody discovers my golden sphere...and me by the same token."

"By trying to kill me with harpoons?"

"These harpoons are harmless. Such 'weapons' can only put you to sleep and magically send you back to where you came from, with no recollection of what happened."

"I see...and the water? How come it's so hot?"

"Right under my hideout, there is an active volcano that erupts through the side of the Himalayan mountains you saw. It really heats up the place!"

"Very interesting! So...what did you want to talk to me about?"

"About your current task, *Chosen One.* I applaud you for all the incredibly difficult missions you have accomplished so far, and admire your great courage and dedication. I wanted to warn you of a great danger I saw in your future."

"What danger?" you ask perplexed.

"The unexpected."

"I know," you tell Pelmut. "The High Priest of Tibet always tells me to expect the unexpected in all situations...and not to ever be surprised."

"He is correct," replies the old man, "but in this particular mission, all sorts of unpredictable dangers will wait to hunt you down...like never before!"

"I'm aware of that."

"Are you really? You don't know the twins Sunita and Raju. They are extremely dangerous, especially Raju. You can't trust him. Watch out for yourself at all times with him. Otherwise, he might literally stab you in the back when you least expect it!"

"Thank you for the advice."

"On top of that, I see so many traps, hooligans, and dangers coming your way. Be aware of your surrounding at all times! If not, a very dark path awaits you."

"I am taking your words very seriously Pelmut."

"You have to, *Chosen One.* Your life will be in constant danger...day and night. Beware! I just wanted to warn you..."

"Thank you for wanting to help me. I must go now."

"Are you sure you don't want any stew? There's nothing else like it!"

"I'm sure. Goodbye Pelmut. Wish me luck!"

Now find Gutuk in section 40

167

You blindly run to your left, and swiftly reach the left wall. Around you, you hear rocks, stalactites, and boulders smashing to the ground and breaking into pieces. But surprisingly, the earthquake is over in no time.

"I was very lucky," you say out loud.

You choose to take a few steps forward and notice that the air suddenly feels thicker...and that the ground is warm!

"What is happening?"

Hastily, you stop walking after suddenly stepping into some hot water! Instinctively, you squat down to touch the liquid...

"I don't understand how this is possible: hot water inside a Himalayan cave?!"

As you say these words, a powerful lantern on a wooden stool magically lights up about fifty feet in front of you. On the other side, you notice a very large body of water in front of which you are standing!

"What in the world is going on?" you say out loud. *"What is this place?"*

Abruptly, a strong pair of hands grab you from behind, and throw you into the water! You immediately expected to hit the ground but you don't because the water is shockingly so deep. You emerge your head out of the water and see four women dressed in tight black diving suits. They all stare at you, and each one is holding a harpoon! The lady who threw you into the water is now aiming at you with her weapon, and sharply says:

"We don't like strangers...so you're history!"

If you are an eternal breath master, dive into section **164**

If you are not, good luck in section **173**!

168

You look at everyone around you, at all of this incredible wealth and opulence, realizing that it is all an illusion about to disappear.

"It's time to call Manna," you tell yourself.

You pull Raju closer to Sunita and say:

"Manna...I have found the twins and we are ready to go see Gutuk. Please come to me..."

A few seconds later, Manna appears in front of you...with her granddaughter! With great smiles, they both walk up to you. Manna takes your hand, and says:

"Hello *Chosen One*. It is so great to see you again!"

"Hi Manna. It is so great to see you too!"

"You recognize my granddaughter Shirisha...she is now healed...thanks to you."

"I'm so happy to see you back on your feet, Shirisha."

"It's all thanks to you, *Chosen One*. I will be eternally grateful."

"I see that there was some serious action around here," says Manna.

"You could say that," you humbly reply.

"I believe that this young lady lying close to you is Sunita...and that this young man is her brother Raju," continues Manna.

"Yes...these are the twins we talked about," you tell Manna.

"What a shame that they chose a dark path in life. They will now have to find another one."

"Indeed Manna."

"It is now time to travel back to Gutuk. Shirisha will accompany us. I will put my hand on your forehead while you touch the twins' heads."

"Understood," you say.

Gently, Manna puts her hand on your forehead while you place your hands on top of the twins' heads.

You close your eyes, and feel a delicate energy flowing from Manna's hand onto your forehead. A few seconds later, you recognize once again the sensation of your body floating on a very soft cloud, rocking you like a gentle sea. All sorts of pleasant images once again appear in your head. A moment later, you find yourself back inside the akashic records...next to Gutuk!

Prepare yourself for section 171

169

"If I am right next to this cave, I might as well take a quick look inside."
You approach the large opening with the feeling that you are just about to be swallowed by a giant mouth. Nevertheless, you step inside the cave...
"It's very dark in here. I don't see much but the light of day does help a little..."

If you master the owl's eye skill, prepare your sight for section 174

If you don't have the above skill, keep walking to section 160

170

You dash towards and jump inside the small opening to your left. It looks more like a tall crack in the wall, but it allows you to safely hide from the turmoil around you. Unexpectedly, the earthquake is over a short moment later. You come out of the opening before saying:
"That could have been much worse," you tell yourself, feeling lucky.
You keep walking straight ahead, and can't help but notice that it's slowly getting warmer in this cave. The air suddenly feels thicker, and the ground is warm!
"What is going on?"
Abruptly, you have to stop walking. In front of you, a very large body of water stretches out for about fifty feet, completely covering the rocky ground. But on the other side of this body of water, you notice a little lantern left on a wooden stool!
"How is this possible? Who could have left a lit lantern in a Himalayan cave?"
Instinctively, you squat down to touch the water...
"I can't believe it! The water is very warm!"
Out of the blue, a strong pair of hands grab you from behind, and throw you into the water! To your surprise, you don't feel the rocky ground under the water because it is so deep. You emerge your head out of the water and see four women, dressed in tight black diving suits. They are all staring at you, and each is holding a harpoon! The lady who threw you in the water is now aiming at you with her weapon, and declares:
"Goodbye, stranger."

If you are an eternal breath master, dive into section **164**

If you are not, good luck in section **173!**

171

Levitating a few feet above the ground, in his immaculate white robe, Gutuk greets you, Manna, and Shirisha with a warm smile.

"Oh! What a beautiful surprise! My heart is filled with joy to see you all! Manna, it has been too long since we have seen each other."

"Time always goes by so fast," answers Manna as she embraces her old friend.

"Shirisha! You are healed and back on your feet. What a great relief to see you like this!"

"Yes Gutuk. It's mainly thanks to the help of *The Chosen One*," tells him Shirisha.

He turns to you, takes both of your hands, and simply says with tears in his eyes:

"I knew it, *Chosen One.* I knew you would succeed in all your endeavors."

"I'm just glad I had Manna and Shirisha by my side to find you now," you humbly respond.

Gutuk peeks at the unconscious twins, who are placed in a sitting position, before saying:

"It's time. I must now reset all time capsules to their original state. This way, everything on Earth will go back to the way it was before any of the time capsule alterations."

"Gutuk," says Manna, "Shirisha and I will now leave you to allow you to finish what you and *The Chosen One* have started. We will come back and visit you in a few days."

"Thank you Manna for all your help. I will see you both very soon."

Both ladies now turn to you with a majestic smile, and Shirisha pats you on the shoulder:

"Goodbye, *Chosen One.* Thank you once again for saving my life."

"I'm so happy I was able to help you," you tell the young lady.

"Promise me that you will visit us in Kathmandu," says Manna.

"I promise," you answer with a smile.

They slowly disappear before your eyes, leaving a serene feeling of love in your heart.

Gutuk sits down, and invites you to do the same.

"I will now place my hand on your forehead to join my spirit with yours, while you touch the twins' heads. Our combined strengths will allow me to forever block them from entering any time capsule, at their own will."

As you touch the twins' heads, Gutuk delicately places his hand on your forehead. You then feel a warm and pleasant current going through your forehead, into your entire body, and into your hands. Suddenly you hear familiar voices:

"What's tickling my head? What's happening?" says a now fully awake Raju.

"Where are we?" adds a now conscious Sunita.

Slowly, the twins try to get up!

**If you want to stop them from getting up,
run as fast as you can to section 161**

If you prefer ignoring them, go to section 175

172

Blindly, you start running to your right towards the wall, hoping to find some sense of orientation when you reach it...but you will never make it. Since you cannot see where you are going, it's impossible for you to avoid falling into a very deep crevasse. Unfortunately, you will not survive such a surprise from Mother Nature. Your mission is over...and our world will soon turn into a masquerade, orchestrated by two self-centered teenagers. Your choices were not very wise...and very costly!

THE END

173

Instinct. The lady is aiming her harpoon at you and she shoots, but you catch the steel arrow in mid-air. Three other dangerous projectiles fly your way but once again, you catch each one of them with great dexterity.

"I should be safe for at least a short while now."

Swiftly, you start swimming under water and away from these crazy divers. In no time, you feel the need to come back to the surface and breathe. When you do, you realize that you have already reached the other side of the large body of warm water! You pull yourself out...and immediately feel a metallic object pressing against your spine.

"Get up and turn around slowly," says an authoritative female voice behind you. You do as you are told, and see four more female divers aiming their harpoons at you.

"Not again," you tell the agile diver.

At that moment, a giant sphere of golden light comes out of the water and illuminates the entire cave! Immediately, all the divers put their weapons down as they now stare at the sphere. The enormous object slowly flies out of the water...in your direction. A moment later, you feel sucked in, and you disappear inside the sphere!

Reappear at section 166!

174

"Thanks to my Tibetan training, seeing in the dark is not a problem for me. It's like having night vision!"

Piercing the darkness with your sharp eyes, you continue walking forward. The cave you are in is immense, and its walls are covered with grey boulders. You look up and notice giant pointy stalactites hanging from the ceiling.

"These stalactites are dangerous," you tell yourself. *"If one of them would fall straight at me…"*

As the thought crosses your mind, the entire cave starts to shake. You see big rocks starting to detach from the walls, before rolling down.

"Oh no! An earthquake!" you say out loud. At the same time, you notice a small opening inside the wall to your left.

If you choose to run to your right to get away from the threatening stalactites hanging over your head, hurry to section 163

If you prefer running towards the small opening to your left, do it at section 170

175

You decide to keep your hands on the twins' heads. They try to get up but you gently push them back down.

"What's going on?" says Sunita. "Where are we?"

"HEY! STOP PRESSING DOWN ON MY HEAD!"

Gutuk's eyes suddenly dive into yours. A tremendous smile covers his face as he tells you:

"It's done, *Chosen One*. You have succeeded in your mission!"

"Chosen what?" says an irritated Raju.

He springs back to his feet, and stares at Gutuk.

"YOU AGAIN? WHO ARE YOU OLD MAN? WHY ARE YOU HERE? WHY ARE WE HERE?"

Sunita gets up, and turns towards you:

"Did this man just call you *Chosen One?*"

"Yes he did," you answer the sister.

"Why? Isn't your name Cho?"

"That's why I asked you and Raju to call me *Cho*: it's short for *Chosen One*."

"Hey! I see that Cho is not at all who we thought!!" yaps Raju. "Cho is a dangerous fakir with super magical powers…and made the golden crown disappear, so that we no longer have it!"

Immediately, Sunita asks you in a vacillating voice:

"Cho…is it true? Did you make the golden crown disappear?"

"Yes I did. Let me explain why I did so…"

Confused, Sunita turns to Gutuk and says:

"I remember you, Sir. You were levitating above the ground the day my brother and I entered a time capsule for the first time."

"That is true, young lady," answer Gutuk with an honest smile.

"May I ask who you are?" continues the young woman.

"Certainly. My name is Gutuk and I am the gate keeper of time. I am responsible for supervising all the events that have ever happened on Earth so far. In other words, I safeguard all the time capsules, each one always recorded by the universe."

"I see. So why am I here with my brother?"

"Young lady, you and your brother have greatly abused the privilege you were given: to travel back in time. You both stole a great deal of wealth from all centuries. You took part in countless fights, hurting many people, with the sole purpose of getting rich. You bought off government officials in Kathmandu in order to eventually take over the entire regime. Your vision for Nepal was that of an absolute dictatorship, and not a democracy. Should I continue?"

"No..." says an embarrassed Sunita.

"Hey sister, let's get out of here and transport ourselves into a time capsule. We don't need to talk to these people. Meet me at our secret hideout."

A moment later, the twins are still standing next to you and Gutuk.

"HEY! WHAT'S GOING ON? WHY ARE WE STILL HERE? SUNITA, HOW COME YOU AND I AREN'T ABLE GO TO THE TIME CAPSULE OF OUR CHOICE?"

"Calm down," says Sunita. "I think I understand what's going on..."

"Please let me confirm it, young lady: your brother and yourself have been forever banned from travelling through time..."

"WHAT?" barks Raju.

He tries to throw a right hook at Gutuk but a superior force stops him, not allowing him to perform such an aggressive action. The old man then tells him:

"Raju, it's time to stop your foolish games, your rudeness, and your inappropriate vocabulary. If you don't stop, I will make you lose your voice for a few days."

The teenager bites his tongue, crosses his arms, and puts his head down. Sunita turns to you and asks:

"Why did we ever cross paths...*Chosen One*? So you could deceive my brother and me?"

"No Sunita. Take a step back for a moment and look at what you have accomplished. Are you proud of yourself? Are you happy that so many people from the past suffered because of you? You stole their wealth, and ruined their lives. What about people on Earth? You have made so many bad decisions, so many wrong choices...and for what? Wealth? Power? Was it worth it?"

The young woman quietly looks down without answering.

"My mission was to bring you both back to Gutuk. In order to do so, I had to stay close to both of you. I learned to tolerate you, and appreciate your differences. Unfortunately, because of the greed in your hearts and the lack of consideration for the suffering of others, you won't be able to travel back in time anymore."

"As we speak," continues Gutuk, "I have reset all time capsules to their original state. In other words, everything on Earth is now back to the way it was before both of you started to alter time capsules."

"So our palace in Kathmandu is gone?" asks Raju.

"Yes it is."

"What about our parents?" adds Sunita. "Are they...alive?"

"No...they are not."

The young woman falls to her knees and starts crying. You feel her tremendous pain as you see big tears rolling down her cheeks.

"I don't want to live like this anymore!" says the young woman. "I lived without my parents for so many years! I missed my mom and my dad every day. I need their love, their guidance, their help. I'm not ready to face the world by myself. I still have so much to learn! I need my parents in my life!"

As all these words come out of Sunita's delicate mouth, Raju sits down next to his sister... and comforts her with a brotherly embrace. Silently, he starts crying with her. After about a minute, he finds the strength and courage to tell Gutuk:

"I agree with my sister. I too need my parents to take care of me, to love me unconditionally, and to guide me. I don't want to have to suddenly live without them...like it happened years ago after the deadly avalanche."

Very surprised by hearing such wise words coming from both brother and sister, Gutuk observes them for a moment. He then looks at you...before glancing at the twins one more time:

"Sunita...Raju...your wise words have touched me deeply. After what I have witnessed from you before this exact moment, I was not expecting to hear such kind and sincere words from the heart."

Gutuk stops floating and stands in front of the twins. He motions them to get up, then he tells them:

"I have decided the following: in order for you to be with your parents, I could personally send you inside a time capsule where you would permanently live with your mother and father. The life you could have now is the same life you had before you entered your first time capsule. You will be able to live a peaceful life, filled with unconditional love, with your parents by your side. What do you say to such a proposition?"

Sunita wraps her arms around Gutuk, like a little girl hugging her grandpa, as she lets big tears slide down her now pinkish cheeks.

"Yes Gutuk...we accept your proposition. It's more than generous. Thank you a thousand times!"

Raju can't find the words to acknowledge his sister's decision, so he simply wraps his arms around her, letting a few tears come out. Finally he finds the strength to say:

"Thank you Gutuk...and I'm sorry for everything I said and did before."

Both twins turn towards you, and Sunita says:

"Cho...I mean *Chosen One*...you reminded us of what is really important in life: not all the riches in the world, not the power, but love and family..."

"...and friends," continues Raju. "You were a good friend...still are...and you saved our lives!"

"That's what friends are for," you respond to them.

"I will never forget how you helped us...and saved us...in so many ways. If someday you want to find us, you know where we are!"

"I sure do," you simply answer as Sunita.

"By the way, where and how did you master all these incredible magical skills you have?"

"It's a long story Raju..."

"So maybe someday..."

"Someday..." you answer him.

"It's time to go back and be with your parents," says Gutuk. "Have a safe trip...and have the best possible life!"

"Thank you Gutuk," they both answer, as they stare at you.

Gutuk smiles at them one last time, and puts his hands on their foreheads. Slowly, the twins disappear before your eyes...through the hallways of time...into a world where their parents are still alive and waiting for them. Gutuk slowly turns around, starts to float again, and asks you:

"So what's next for you, *Chosen One*?"

"Well, I will first pay a little visit to some new friends in Kathmandu. Then, I will participate in a martial arts tournament in Japan with my friend Kenji-san."

"That sounds very exciting! Please send my best regards to Manna and Shirisha."

"I will Gutuk."

As you shake hands, he tells you:

"Thank you for helping out with the twins. They are good youngsters but they needed you to lead them back onto the right life path."

"I'm glad it all worked out in the end."

"You know where to find me..."

"I do Gutuk. I will see you soon."

...and you slowly disappear before his eyes...

CONGRATULATIONS!

YOU HAVE COMPLETED

YOUR

MISSION!

NOW

GET READY

FOR YOUR

NEXT MISSION!

YOUR NEXT ADVENTURE

AWAITS YOU…

ABOUT THE AUTHOR

As a young boy, Jeff Storm did not really enjoy reading. He could not relate to most books offered to him and quickly got bored reading them. One day his mother introduced him to all sorts of action packed books written by the elusive French writer Henri Vernes and the American icon Robert Ludlum. Jeff was hooked. He loved the martial arts sequences, the good triumphing over evil, and the bandits being stopped. He felt a strong connection to the stories, sometimes imagining he was the hero catching the bad guys. As he read those books, he had a vision: someday, he would start his own collection of books where the reader is the hero of the story... and he did, adding many incredible twists to his outstanding and unique work!

Besides being a passionate writer, Jeff Storm is a dedicated teacher with many years of experience under his belt. "I love children and find that every day, I am learning something new from them. If I can inspire my students to use their creativity and imagination in a positive way in order to reach their personal goals and have the success they want, I have done my job."

Jeff Storm may be contacted on:

Website
www.jeff-storm.com

Facebook
Jeff Storm Kids Books

Instagram
@jeffstormkidsbooks

Twitter
@jeffstormbooks

CPSIA information can be obtained
at www.ICGtesting.com
Printed in the USA
LVOW07s1543041017
551170LV00011B/1022/P